His hands moved to cup her face and he lowered his own mouth to hers. By the time he brushed her lips, she was struggling for breath. By the time he kissed her, she was unable to think clearly. Celia gasped as his mouth took hers. His soft, mesmerizing words had clouded her brain. His lips, hungry and searching, made her go limp. She felt his arms reach around to steady her, felt him pull her close, felt her own lips offering themselves to him . . . and then suddenly she was on her feet, backing away from him, her eyes brimming, then overflowing with tears. . . .

By Lois Menzel
Published by Fawcett Books:

IN THE SHADOW OF ARABELLA
CELIA

CELIA

Lois Menzel

FAWCETT CREST • NEW YORK

A Fawcett Crest Book
Published by Ballantine Books
Copyright © 1995 by Lois Menzel

All rights reserved under International and Pan-American Copyright Conventions. Published in the United States by Ballantine Books, a division of Random House, Inc., New York, and simultaneously in Canada by Random House of Canada Limited, Toronto.

Library of Congress Catalog Card Number: 95-90143

ISBN 0-449-22342-6

Manufactured in the United States of America

First Edition: August 1995

10 9 8 7 6 5 4 3 2 1

For Carol, Connie, Corinne, Isabel,
Joan, Karen, and Marjorie

Come my Celia, let us prove,
While we may, the sports of love;
Time will not be ours, for ever:
He, at length, our good will sever.
Spend not then his gifts in vain.
Suns, that set, may rise again:
But if once we lose this light,
'Tis, with us, perpetual night.
    —Ben Jonson, "Song. To Celia."

Chapter 1

ALTHOUGH IT WAS close on one o'clock in the morning, light shown from nearly every window of Devonshire House. Inside the massive ballroom, the light and heat of several hundred candles poured down upon the assembly. The brightly clad ladies and soberly hued gentlemen were neatly coupled, dancing to the melodious strains of Schubert. The waltz, a few years earlier considered shockingly foreign and indecent, was now widely performed and accepted, even within the revered halls of Almack's Assembly Rooms.

Mrs. Lavinia Demming sat at the edge of the room and observed the dancers with rapt attention. She did not notice the heat nor the tightness of a too-small pair of slippers she had chosen to wear. She did note, however, that Miss Roper looked sick in pink, that Mr. Severson was dancing for the second time with a chit from the Harris brood, that Miss Mablethorpe was not as beautiful as everyone had been led to believe, and that Viscount Moorcroft was smiling in a most possessive way at his partner, the daughter of the Earl of Siddons.

Mrs. Demming's sharp ears listened with a rabbit's attention to all comments that came her way. She heard a lady two seats from her comment that Lord Trevanian had finally arrived at the ball. Another woman strolling by was heard to say that Lady Elliot was increasing.

Leaving off her observation of Viscount Moorcroft and his partner, Mrs. Demming sought her own child among the dancers. Noticing first the pale green gown and then the unmistakable auburn curls of her youngest daughter, Mrs. Demming smiled with contentment.

For the past ten years she had been consumed by one occupation: securing suitable, unexceptionable, advantageous matches for her daughters. Amelia, Dorothea, Melinda, and Sophia were all safely wed. Only Celia remained—her youngest and, some would argue, loveliest child.

As the music ended, Celia's partner gallantly returned her to her mother's side. Celia smiled and curtsied as she thanked him for the dance.

"The pleasure was all mine, Miss Demming," he replied as he bowed, smiled at her mother, then turned away.

"A very pretty performance, child," her mother approved when the gentleman was out of earshot. She spoke quietly, knowing that others were always listening. "Lord Arlington has ten thousand a year, a handsome estate in Suffolk."

"He is very shy, Mama."

"I find shyness becoming in a gentleman. Too many men are bold as brass these days. Lord Trevanian is here."

Celia allowed herself a sideways glance at her mother. "He does not admire me, Mama."

"Nonsense. All men admire you. What is there not to admire? If he cares not for your person, then perhaps your fortune will attach him. If he should ask you to dance, you must do your utmost to please him."

"Yes, Mama."

"You are flushed, child. Fan yourself."

Celia unfurled her fan as her mother bade her and began gently to cool her face. "It is stifling in here. I had not expected such a huge crowd, especially during the Little Season."

"Spirits were low in the spring with all the talk of war," her mother replied. "No one felt much like dancing, with Bonaparte marching across France. Now that we are safe from him at last, all wish to celebrate. It appears as if everyone has come to Town; it will be a wonderful opportunity for you."

Another thirty minutes passed, but Lord Trevanian did not approach them. Celia danced again and was once more seated with her mother when her attention was drawn to a young man standing in conversation nearby. She watched him openly, admiring his trim figure and handsomely tanned face. He was tall with slightly curling light brown hair. When he laughed at something his companion said, his smile was devastating.

"Who is the gentleman speaking with Lord Roth?" she asked her mother quietly. "I don't believe I have ever seen him before."

Mrs. Demming followed the direction of her daughter's gaze. When she replied, her tone held an approving note, and Celia was relieved. She had learned from past experience that disapproval in her mother's voice denoted either a married man or one who was totally unsuitable for any of a score of reasons, ranging from lack of money to lack of connections.

"That is Anthony Graydon, younger son of the Earl of Walsh. I am surprised to see him here. I had understood he was in Belgium, searching for his elder brother."

"Searching?"

"Viscount Wexford fought at Waterloo. He was attached to Lord Uxbridge, I believe. He has been missing since the battle."

"Missing? You mean he was killed?"

"So it is assumed. Yet they have not recovered his body."

"Perhaps he was buried in one of the common graves."

"It's not likely that they would cast a colonel into a common grave."

"But if he's not dead, where could he be?"

"God only knows, child. Perhaps he is dead, buried almost anywhere. Perhaps his brother has found him. Since we cannot walk over and ask him, we must wait to see what the grapevine yields."

While her mother spoke, Celia regarded the gentleman with growing interest. Just then he glanced in her direction, and instinctively she smiled at him. Then she blushed at her own boldness and turned her face away.

* * *

"During the month of July, I searched every hospital and rehabilitation facility," Anthony Graydon said to his companion. "I found nothing. In August, I decided to go to Belgium and try there."

"And had you any luck?" Lord Roth asked.

"No. None. There is no trace of him."

As Anthony glanced past Lord Roth, he noticed a remarkably lovely young woman sitting at the side of the room regarding him. She smiled at him in so friendly a manner that he wondered for a moment if they were acquainted. After she looked away, he regarded her a moment longer. Her skin was pale and delicate. Her hair was dressed fashionably, with a few curling tendrils allowed to escape to lie shining on her shoulders. He glanced briefly at the woman beside her—no doubt her mother. He did not know her.

"I have not danced all evening, Roth. Are you acquainted with the lady in violet, beside the young lady in green?"

Lord Roth turned to see to whom Anthony referred and answered, "That's Lavinia Demming; the girl is her youngest. Should you like an introduction?"

"Very much so," Anthony answered.

"Come along then, but be on your best behavior. The mother is a high stickler."

Introductions having been properly made, Anthony Graydon asked Miss Demming if she would care to stand up with him. With her mother's permission, they moved off to join in a set of country-dances.

Separated by the movements of the dance, they

5

had little opportunity for speech. Delighted by Miss Demming's proficiency on the floor, Anthony smiled his pleasure. Each time he smiled at her, she responded in kind.

At the edge of the room, Mrs. Demming watched the couple for a few moments, then turned to study other faces that were watching them as well. She sat up straighter and allowed a pleased smile to settle on her countenance.

Celia rose at ten o'clock the following morning and spent one full hour in careful preparation before presenting herself downstairs. Diligent attention to one's appearance was one of Mrs. Demming's cardinal rules and one that Celia never considered breaking. Since one never knew who might call or whom one might encounter during the day's activities, it was prudent to look one's best at all times.

When Celia descended, she found her elder sister Dorothea and Dorothea's husband, Mr. Edgehill, seated with her mother in the breakfast parlor.

She arrived in time to hear her mother ask, "And did you happen to see, Dotty, with whom Celia shared the last set of the evening?"

"Indeed we did," Dorothea responded. "I didn't realize you were acquainted with the Graydon family."

"Nor am I. *He* sought the introduction."

As Celia filled her plate from a selection of dishes on the sideboard, taking only eggs and toast, Mr. Edgehill added, "He's recently back from the Continent."

Mrs. Demming turned her gaze upon her son-in-law. "So I had heard, Howard. Tell me, how did his journey fare?"

"He found no trace of Wexford, if that's what you mean. Awkward situation for him, I should think. Most likely Wexford is dead, but it would be simpler for Graydon to succeed if there were some proof."

Celia seated herself at the table and accepted the cup of tea her sister had poured for her.

"The Earl of Walsh suffered an apoplexy in the spring, and his condition has deteriorated steadily since," Dorothea said. "He is bedridden at his home in Buckinghamshire. No one expects him to live long, poor man. I think it's a blessing that he will never know of Wexford's death."

"You think he is dead, then, Dotty?" Celia asked.

"He must be, or surely he would have been found by now. It's been three months since Waterloo!"

Mr. Edgehill soon departed, saying he had an appointment to keep. While the conversation shifted to other items of gossip, Celia carefully spread blackberry jam on a piece of toast and for a moment permitted herself to speculate. Mr. Graydon had sought an introduction and had danced with her. He had also complimented her on her gown—something he was not obliged to do. Perhaps it was mere gallantry—or perhaps ... Dorothea and Sophia had married commoners, though they were both of good family with respectable fortunes. Melinda had wed a knight, and Amelia a baronet, both pleasing their mama by becoming ladies. If Mr. Graydon was interested ... and if his brother was indeed dead . . . and if she could somehow manage to attach him . . . she could someday be a countess!

What joy would be hers if she could accomplish this noble feat! All her life she had been made to fetch and carry by her sisters. All her life she had been last: last to put up her hair, last to have long dresses and jewelry, last to go to parties, last to be brought out. If she could manage in the end to be first in rank, much could be atoned for.

She had to abandon her grandiose dreams when she realized her sister was asking her what she intended to wear to the Effinghams' ball on Saturday.

Though she asked the question of Celia, both Dotty and Celia looked to their mother for the answer, for Celia never chose any gown herself; the choice was always Lavinia's.

"I did think she should wear the turquoise satin," their mother replied, "since I believe it to be Trevanian's favorite color. But I wonder . . . perhaps the white would be more appropriate in the event Mr. Graydon should be present."

Lavinia Demming stepped back to regard her daughter with a critical eye. The gown was an excellent choice. White crepe over white satin, it accentuated Celia's flawless complexion and contrasted sharply with her luxurious hair. How fortunate, Lavinia thought, that the girl should be blessed with that bold touch of red in her dark curls, a trait that set her apart from other dark women. A simple strand of pearls, matching ear bobs, long white gloves, a chicken-skin fan, and a dainty reticule studded with seed pearls completed Celia's ensemble.

As they mounted the grand staircase at Lord and Lady Effingham's home, Lavinia whispered last-minute instructions to her daughter. "If by some good fortune Mr. Graydon should approach us again, mind each word you say, Celia. Do nothing that might offend. Smile. And answer his questions with good sense. He does not strike me as a man who would appreciate a ninnyhammer. He's an out-and-outer, make no mistake, but you are handsome enough to turn any head. If you were to take his fancy, it would please me no end."

Celia said nothing and allowed herself to hope. Since her come-out, she'd had many admirers and two offers of marriage. The proposals had been politely refused, for although both suitors were young and personable, they were also poor as church mice and therefore considered by Mrs. Demming to be fortune hunters. Celia was twenty, and she knew that many other girls her age were already married or at least engaged. Perhaps Mr. Graydon would be the man in her future.

Anthony Graydon did approach the Demming ladies again. He was one of the first gentlemen to greet them after they had gained the ballroom. When he asked Celia to save the first waltz for him, she had no need to remember her mother's admonitions, for her smile was spontaneous.

Anthony Graydon had been enchanted with Miss Demming at their first meeting and was looking forward to seeing her again. He found her fragile beauty intriguing and wondered why he had never noticed her before. While he marked time, waiting for their promised dance, he anticipated how she would feel in his arms.

As they took the floor together, he said, "Since we met the other evening, Miss Demming, I have been wondering what your given name is. Might I know it, or will you consider me too bold?"

"It is Celia, sir, and I do not think your question bold." She glanced up into his face and found his blue eyes twinkling with amusement.

" 'Come my Celia, let us prove . . .' "

Clearly puzzled by the rejoinder, she asked, "Excuse me, sir?"

"It's a piece of a poem—by Ben Jonson. Do you know it?"

"No, sir, I don't."

"It's a fine name. It suits you."

"Thank you, sir."

Several minutes passed in silence before he spoke again. "You dance delightfully, Miss Demming."

"Thank you, sir. I'm pleased that you think so."

"Do you realize that each time I speak, you thank me?"

"Each time you speak you compliment me, sir. It is only proper that I thank you."

"And do you always do what is proper, Miss Demming?"

He was teasing her and was therefore surprised when she answered with perfect gravity. "I try very hard to. Sometimes I fail. It is not always easy to decide what is proper."

"Would you consider it improper for me to ask how old you are?"

He was amused when she considered a moment before answering. "I think your question is rather more indelicate than improper, sir."

"Dear me. I am such a clod. I had not intended to be indelicate, nor to have you think ill of me."

"I think you are curious, Mr. Graydon, and I will strike a bargain with you. I myself have a curious nature. I will tell you what you wish to know, if you will share the same information with me."

"I agree," he said.

"I turned twenty, sir, in July."

"I will be seven and twenty in November." As the final bars of the music played, he asked, "Do you go to the Rutledges' soiree next week?"

"Perhaps" was all she said before he returned her to her mother and took his leave.

Nothing could have exceeded Lavinia Demming's delight when Celia revealed the salient points of her conversation with Mr. Graydon: he had complimented her again; he had asked if she would be at the Rutledge party the following Tuesday. These were wonderful tidings—wonderful tidings, indeed. Mrs. Demming already had an invitation to the Rutledges', but if she hadn't had one, she would have moved heaven and earth to acquire it.

Marriage into the Graydon family would be a victory in itself, but if Viscount Wexford had indeed perished at Waterloo, then young Anthony would be the new earl one day and Lavinia's youngest child would be a countess. She could scarcely believe her good fortune.

On Tuesday night Lavinia selected for Celia a sea-green gown embroidered with gold thread. It was a color that complemented Celia's dark green eyes and brought out the red tones in her hair. Although Lavinia already felt the situation with Graydon was promising, she was always prepared to hedge her bets. He had first noticed Celia in green, perhaps green would please him again.

Celia's sister Amelia and Amelia's husband, Lord William Lane, were also present on Tuesday night. Celia was partnered for nearly every dance. When she sat with her sister and mother during the intervals, she said little.

Finally Amelia commented, "You are very quiet tonight, Celia. Aren't you feeling well?"

"I'm sorry," Celia responded. "Am I being dull?"

"Celia had hoped Mr. Graydon would stand up with her tonight," Lavinia answered quietly. "But we have been here more than two hours and . . ."

"Maybe he hasn't even come," Amelia suggested. "Have you seen him?"

"No," Celia replied, "but he specifically asked me if I would be here tonight, so naturally I thought *he* would be."

Mrs. Demming assumed an offended air. "I pray he is not trifling with you, Celia. I will think much less of him if he is. I do not care for it in the least when gentlemen—" She stopped speaking suddenly, and her demeanor changed from one of haughty disapproval to pleased surprise.

Celia looked up to see Mr. Graydon making his

12

way toward them. Her fit of the sullens fled, to be replaced by a rebirth of hope.

Earlier in the evening she had danced with Mr. Prescott, who had ever so slight a paunch and an unquestionable bald spot, Sir Ralph Hazelwood, charming but over forty, and Lord Sutton, wealthy but humorless.

Compared with these gentlemen, Anthony Graydon was perfection. His black evening coat set off his broad shoulders superbly, and his satin knee breeches did little to hide the strong muscularity of his legs. His curling brown hair, far from showing any sign of thinning, had been ruthlessly brushed into perfect order. His young, rakishly handsome smile was genuine and focused directly upon Celia. When he asked for her company in the dance and her mother nodded approval, Celia placed her small hand in his very large one, her heart thumping uncomfortably within her breast.

As she watched her daughter waltz with Mr. Graydon, Lavinia preened. If Mr. Graydon could be brought up to scratch, this match would be her greatest victory.

Nearly an hour later both Demming ladies retired upstairs to refresh themselves. After Lavinia was satisfied that Celia's slightly dance-tangled curls were once again perfect, they descended the stairway together. When they had come halfway down, Celia noticed Anthony Graydon standing at the bottom of the stairs in conversation with several other gentlemen. Perhaps he had been watching for her, for he looked up at that moment and smiled when he saw her.

Celia thought of all the trips she had made up and down the stairs at her home in Yorkshire with a heavy book on her head. "Keep your chin up, Celia," her governess would say. "And under no circumstances sway your hips. Most unladylike, to be sure."

With hard work and determination, Celia had mastered the balanced book both on the floor and on the stairs. Now Mr. Graydon would be the fortunate recipient of her hard-won poise, her practiced grace. She smiled, parting her lips to allow her perfectly straight teeth to show slightly.

Then, in the twinkling of an eye, she somehow misjudged the next step and was caught off balance. She made a desperate grab for the balustrade, but it was beyond her reach. She had time only to notice a startled look of dismay on Mr. Graydon's face before she tumbled headlong down the remaining ten steps, landing in a heap of arms, legs, sea-green flounces, and exposed petticoats directly at Mr. Graydon's feet.

While Mrs. Demming stood frozen with shock on the stairs, a quick-thinking Anthony bent swiftly to twitch Celia's gown back down over her exposed ankles and frilly white undergarments.

"Are you all right, Miss Demming?" he asked. "Such a nasty fall!"

His tone held genuine concern, but Celia did not hear it. Quickly pulling her legs under her, she accepted Anthony's support to rise to her feet. She was aware that all talking in the hall had ceased and all eyes were upon her. She felt in that instant that she must surely die of shame.

When Anthony once again asked her if she was all right, she mumbled, "I'm fine, sir, thank you. Please excuse me." With her eyes downcast, she moved as quickly as possible toward the cloakroom, wanting only to escape the scene of her disgrace.

Mrs. Demming followed her daughter. As she passed Anthony, he said, "With your permission, Mrs. Demming, I will call in the morning to be sure she wasn't hurt."

"You're very kind, sir," Lavinia replied. "Good night."

It was only after they had gone that he realized he didn't know where they lived.

Chapter 2

LATE THE FOLLOWING morning Anthony Graydon wasted no time in learning the direction of the Demming family. His source of information was Lord Roth.

"Is there a Mr. Demming, Henry?"

"So I understand, though I have never met the gentleman. His property is in Yorkshire, and I believe he prefers the rolling hills to the smoky city. It's said that his flocks produce the best wool in the county. He is rumored to be considerably wealthy. His four older daughters were handsomely dowered, and Miss Celia, so the gossips say, has an equal portion."

"It is not Miss Demming's fortune that concerns me at this moment, Henry. I cannot believe that so frail a creature did not suffer some injury from her fall last night. It was utterly appalling. It happened so quickly, there was nothing I could do. And all those stuffy matrons were standing about. No doubt their tongues are rattling today, eager to spread the tale of someone else's misadventure. They live in Brook Street, you say?"

"Yes. Number seventeen."

"I will call there directly after my stop at the War Office."

"Since you're still going there every day, I assume there has been no word of Wexford."

"No. But I refuse to give up hope."

After hearing at the War Office the same tidings he had heard time and time again, Anthony called in Brook Street and found Mrs. Demming at home. She was alone when he was ushered into a handsomely appointed salon.

"So good of you to call, Mr. Graydon."

"How is your daughter this morning, ma'am? Last night she said she was fine, but I can't help worrying."

"She has a few ugly bruises, I fear, but nothing more serious. No broken bones or anything of that nature."

"I am relieved to hear it, Mrs. Demming, for I must tell you that I feel in some part responsible for this accident."

"Goodness, sir! Certainly not!"

"Indeed," he insisted. "I had caught her eye, and she was looking at me instead of minding her step. If I had not distracted her . . ."

"However that may be, sir, she was not hurt. She is greatly embarrassed, but will overcome that in time."

"I was hoping I could see her this morning," he said.

"She decided not to come down today . . . but perhaps tomorrow . . ." She left the sentence unfinished, clearly an invitation.

17

"I will call again tomorrow, then, madam, if you're sure it's not an imposition."

"We would be delighted, Mr. Graydon."

When he had gone, Lavinia whisked herself up to Celia's room. Celia was still abed, studying fashion plates.

"You will never guess who came to call," Lavinia said as she seated herself in a chair next to the bed.

"I am not in a mood for games, Mama," Celia answered sourly. "If you would simply tell me, there would be no need for me to guess."

"Very well. It was Mr. Anthony Graydon."

Celia's eyes opened wide in astonishment. "You jest, Mama."

"Certainly not. And he asked after you. What's more, he intends to return tomorrow to see for himself that you suffered no harm in your fall."

"My fall? You should say my public disgrace. And he may save himself the trouble of stopping again, for I will not see him!"

"Of course, you will. You cannot hide in your room forever."

"How can I show my face anywhere, Mama? Dozens of people saw me fall, and they must have given an eyewitness account to all their friends. I can't bear to think about it. It's all too awful."

"A few days at home to recover is understandable, Celia, but sooner or later you must enter society again. And if a few people should stare or whisper, let them. All will soon be forgotten."

"I will not forget," Celia cried passionately. "Not ever!"

On Thursday morning Mrs. Demming once more received Mr. Graydon alone, for nothing she could say would budge Celia from her bedchamber. This time he left behind a floral tribute for the young lady: a modest bunch of violet hearts-ease tied with a green ribbon. When Lavinia delivered this to Celia, she burst into tears. Wisely Lavinia decided not to tell her child that the gentleman insisted upon calling yet once again on the following day.

By Friday morning Celia was heartily sick of her room and ventured downstairs for an early breakfast. At precisely twenty-five after eleven, Lavinia asked if Celia would be kind enough to put on a shawl and go out into the garden to see if there were any chrysanthemums that might serve to brighten the sitting room.

A few minutes later Lavinia heard her butler admitting Mr. Graydon in the front hall. She walked there to meet him.

When the butler had left them alone, he said, "I hope you have been able to convince Miss Demming to see me, ma'am."

"I must admit, sir, I have never known my child to be so obstinate as she is being in this instance. I assure you, she is not typically so. I actually believe that if she would speak with you, it would help her get past this terrible embarrassment she is feeling. She is presently in the garden behind the house. Perhaps we should join her there."

Anthony followed her down a short hallway and out a rear door into a neatly landscaped garden with high walls and winding brick paths.

Celia turned when she heard the door closing,

then stood transfixed as she saw who accompanied her mother. If she could have run away, she would have, but they barred the only way back into the house.

In a light conversational tone, Lavinia said unnecessarily, "Look who has come to pay us a call, Celia—Mr. Graydon. I believe I will leave you to entertain him, for I really must have some of the Michaelmas daisies for the dinner table tonight." She casually took the shears from her daughter's unresisting hand, excused herself, and walked away, staying in sight but out of earshot. Anthony walked forward until he was standing within a few feet of Celia.

She felt herself blushing and dropped her gaze, steadfastly regarding the cut flowers in her hands.

"I have called three days in succession hoping to see you," he said. "I wanted to assure myself that you had not been injured, but even more, I wanted to apologize. I believe it was my fault that you fell."

This brought her gaze up to meet his. His face was full of concern, his eyes apologetic. "How could it be your fault?" she asked.

"I caught your eye from the bottom of the stairs. I distracted you. If I have been the cause of any injury to you, I will never forgive myself. I can't begin to tell you how sorry I am. Coming down the stairs—you were so lovely. You *are* so lovely."

Celia blushed anew, not so much affected by the words themselves as by the tone in which he uttered them. His voice was low and full, charged with emotion.

He reached to take her free hand and found it

was cold and shaking. He enclosed it between both of his.

"I was not injured, sir, as you can see. And you were not to blame, please don't think it. It was an accident, nothing more."

Still in an intimate, caressing tone he said, "I have missed seeing you these past several days. Will you come driving with me today—this afternoon?"

As Celia hesitated, her mother sailed back to the couple, and Anthony dropped the young lady's hand. "And have you two been having a cozy chat?"

"We have, ma'am," Anthony replied. "I have asked Miss Celia if she would care to be taken up in my phaeton this afternoon for a turn through Hyde Park."

"Oh, how lovely! But of course she would be delighted, wouldn't you, Celia, darling?"

At this prompting, Celia replied with only a hint of reluctance, "Thank you, sir. I should like it of all things."

When they had set a time and Anthony had departed, Lavinia said, "There now, what could be better? To be seen driving with Mr. Graydon will be a fine feather in your cap, Celia. You will be the envy of half the women in London."

Celia remained unconvinced but later returned from her excursion to the park in high spirits. As Lavinia had guessed, the whispering that Celia feared from society had been outweighed by Mr. Graydon's charm.

Two days later Celia attended a rout at Sir Laurence and Lady Elizabeth Bessinger's. When she and her mother entered the room, there was no question that heads turned and conversation lessened, but when Mr. Anthony Graydon offered Miss Demming his arm into the reception room, the partygoers resumed their earlier conversation.

On the second day of October, Anthony drove from London to his family home near High Wycombe in the Chiltern Hills. Traveling by curricle, he accomplished the journey in under three hours. He was delayed for some minutes in the village of Little Graydon by a herd of cattle that completely blocked the street. When they had cleared, he drove on past the Gothic church with its high, square belfry.

A mile farther on he turned in at the lodge gates of Walsh Priory. Having been added onto several times since its humble priory beginnings in the thirteenth century, it had grown into a massive rectangular structure of mellow, weathered limestone with tall square towers adorning each corner.

Anthony arrived as his mother was enjoying a light luncheon. The Countess of Walsh had turned fifty but looked younger. She retained the tall, slender figure of her youth, and the graying locks at her temples blended subtly into her fair hair. She rose expectantly when he entered the room, for as always when he arrived without notice, she hoped he might have news of her elder son.

He shook his head as he advanced to take her hand. "No, Mother, I'm sorry. There has been no word."

She smiled and gestured to the table spread with

delicate dishes. "Won't you share my luncheon? I love it when you come to visit whether you have news of Robert or not."

"Allow me a moment or two to wash off the dust of the road, and I will be happy to join you."

When he returned to the room some minutes later, he sat beside his mother at one end of the large dining table. "How is Father doing?"

"There has been little change. He eats when he is told and is generally docile and biddable. But he still seems not to know us, and he stares continually into space when he is awake. He sleeps a great deal, of course."

"I'll go up and sit with him for a while after we finish eating."

"I think he will enjoy that, Tony. In fact, I'm certain he will."

"I don't like your being here alone," Anthony said. "I wish you would have someone to stay with you."

"I'm not alone. Ursula rides over from the rectory every day, dear child, and sometimes her mother comes, too. Our neighbors are very attentive, Tony. I have many visitors. But tell me. Had you some purpose in coming today?"

Anthony laid down the knife with which he had cut a slice of beef, then put down the fork as well. "Actually, yes. There was something I wished to discuss with you. Something of import."

"Yes?" she prompted.

"I've met a young woman."

Lady Walsh raised her brows with interest but said nothing.

"Her name is Celia Demming. Her family hails from Yorkshire. Do you know the name?"

"I don't believe so."

"I don't know much myself. Only what Roth has told me. It appears Miss Demming's father is a younger son of some obscure North Country baronet. He inherited a piece of land from an aunt and applied himself to raising sheep. His venture prospered; he acquired more land and apparently made his fortune. He has five daughters, Celia is the youngest."

"How young is that?"

"Twenty. Mrs. Demming has some distant connection to Pembroke through her sister, but otherwise the family is merely respectable."

"Since you are discussing this young woman's background, I assume your interest is serious?"

"Yes, it is."

"What else do you know of her?"

"The rumor mill has it that she is an heiress, but I don't need a dowered wife."

"True. But what exactly is it that you seek from me, Anthony? My blessing?"

"I should like that, of course. But I should like first for you to meet both Miss Demming and her mother. Since you can't come to Town, I thought perhaps you could invite them here for a few days."

"I could easily do that. But tell me: have you already offered for this girl?"

"No."

"You do realize that inviting her here with only her mother and without a larger party of people will have nearly the same effect as a public declaration."

"Yes, I realize that."

"Very well. If this is indeed what you wish, Anthony, I will write the invitation today, and you may carry it back to Town with you."

Nothing could have exceeded Mrs. Demming's glee when Anthony delivered the Countess of Walsh's invitation upon his return to London. Alone with Celia, she could barely contain her excitement.

"I cannot tell you, dear child, how happy you have made me. In a few short weeks, to have attached a gentleman of Graydon's rank—even I, who recognize your excellent qualities, would not have believed it possible. An invitation to Walsh Priory, no less! Dear Celia, how pleased your papa will be!"

"I must admit, I am nervous about meeting the countess," Celia said. "What if she doesn't like me?"

"If you behave as you have been taught, mind your manners and your tongue, she will have no fault to find with you. And you must remember, Celia, it is not so important that she like you, as that she take no dislike to you."

"Do you think we will be asked to meet the earl?"

"I can't say, Celia. I don't know if he sees visitors. But if Mr. Graydon should ask you to visit with his father, of course, you must do so."

A frown clouded Celia's face. "But you know how much I dislike sickrooms, Mama. I feel uncomfortable around old people, especially those who are ill."

"Then you must subdue those feelings, Celia. It is only proper for those who enjoy health and youth to have compassion for others less fortunate. And you must do what is proper—always. There is no other acceptable behavior."

Mrs. Demming packed for the visit with great care, choosing modest gowns that would appeal to the countess and at the same time selecting colors that would show Celia to her best advantage.

They departed London in mid-October, making the journey by post chaise and arriving at Little Graydon without incident. Since the Demming ladies had no male relative available to accompany them, Anthony had insisted upon riding alongside their carriage as escort.

When the Demmings arrived at Walsh Priory, Lady Walsh received them with every outward appearance of pleasure. Anxious for acceptance, Celia studied the countess carefully, trying to determine if the smile of greeting was sincere or merely a facade. It seemed genuine—warm and welcoming— and Celia relaxed. After brief introductions were made, the Demming ladies were shown to their rooms—luxurious, airy apartments where every comfort had been considered.

In Celia's room the bed was hung in dark green silk, while the coverlet was white with green embroidered edges. The draperies were open to their fullest extent, allowing maximum penetration from a cloud-shrouded sun. A large fire in the grate dispelled the chill. Within a few moments a young chambermaid appeared with hot water and warmed towels.

Lavinia, who never budged from her home without Wylie, her personal maid, sent this skilled domestic to Celia's room as soon as she herself had finished dressing for dinner. Wylie arranged Celia's hair, then assisted her to step into the gown Lavinia had chosen. Modestly cut from pale blue crepe, it had two simple flounces and long sleeves with buttoned cuffs—a perfect gown for forming first impressions. Celia was ready and waiting by the time the dinner gong sounded. She met her mother in the hall outside her room, and they descended the stairs together.

As the dinner progressed, the Countess of Walsh allowed herself to release some of the tension that had been building within her throughout the days preceding Celia Demming's visit.

It had not been an easy year for her. Her husband's collapse in the spring, followed by Robert's departure with the army and his subsequent disappearance, had shaken her well-patterned life to its center. Anthony was the only constant that remained to her, and the thought that her relationship with him might be threatened filled her with anxiety.

It wasn't that she didn't wish Anthony to marry—she did. But she knew that his choice of a wife was a decision that must be made with infinite care. The wrong woman could make him unhappy for the rest of his days.

It seemed to her that his attraction for Miss Demming had sprung from nowhere, almost overnight. An infatuation for a woman he barely knew was not, in Lady Walsh's estimation, a good basis for a declaration of marriage. Yet Anthony had already admitted that it was marriage he was considering.

So the countess had waited for the visit of Miss Demming with carefully concealed apprehension. Now as the meal progressed, she allowed herself to breathe easier, for although she found the mother to be somewhat common, the young lady was unexceptionable. She was certainly lovely, poised, not at all shy, but not haughty, either. She seemed intelligent, and some of her comments suggested a lively curiosity.

The conversation had turned to hunting, and Lady Walsh offered, "Anthony took a terrible fall last winter. Broke his arm when the horse rolled on him. Do you hunt, Miss Demming?"

"No, Lady Walsh, I'm afraid I don't."

"And why is that?" Anthony asked.

"I say that it is because I feel sorry for the fox," Celia replied, "but the real reason is that I am a mediocre rider at best, and I'm not fond of jumping."

Lady Walsh regarded her son carefully to see what kind of reaction this confession would bring from a man who loved hunting as he loved life. He was smiling. She could see disbelief and perhaps some disappointment there, but no disillusionment.

When Anthony said nothing, Lavinia added, "In truth, Celia rides quite well, and she can drive a four-in-hand."

Lady Walsh's eyebrows rose with interest as Anthony said, "Indeed. And who taught you that trick?"

"My father. He's an excellent whip. For as long as I can remember, I have always preferred driving to riding."

"You must take me up one day, Miss Demming," the countess said. "I don't get out enough, and I do so enjoy an open carriage."

At the end of two days, the countess felt as if she had known Celia for weeks. There was no pretense about the girl. She was charming.

On the morning of the third day, Lady Walsh encountered Celia in the upstairs hallway, greeted her, then followed her greeting with a question. "I am going to sit with my husband, Miss Demming. Should you like to accompany me?"

Celia had dreaded this moment, but she had also prepared herself for it. She answered smiling and without hesitation. "I should very much like to meet the earl."

The countess smiled sadly in reply. "You understand that it will not be a conventional meeting in any sense. My husband does not speak, nor does he seem to see anything, though his eyes are open. I believe, however, that he can hear us, and that he is simply unable to respond."

As she followed Lady Walsh into the earl's bedchamber, Celia fought the growing feeling of unease in the pit of her stomach. She had never been able to abide sick people. Being near old people made her uncomfortable. She didn't like to look at them and never knew what to say when they spoke to her, especially when their speech was irrational or difficult to understand. She couldn't bear to look at the mutilated soldiers who had returned from Belgium with missing arms or legs, severed hands, or horrible scarring.

She stood beside the bed and smiled into Lord Walsh's vacant face as she was introduced. He appeared to be much older than Lady Walsh.

As if she had read Celia's mind, the countess said, "My husband is nearly twenty years older than I, Miss Demming, but was active and healthy up until the very day he became ill. Only the day before, we had danced at a ball until three in the morning. He is a wonderful dancer." Then, seeming to recollect herself, she said, "Thank you for coming with me, dear, but I think you must be on your way. Anthony will be waiting to take you driving."

When Celia reached the door, she paused to look back. Lady Walsh had taken a chair near the head of the bed and was speaking earnestly to her husband while his unresponsive hand rested in her own.

Chapter 3

ANTHONY ALLOWED HIS horses to walk along the narrow track that wound its way into a fold of the hills. A small stream tripped by in the opposite direction as they slowly climbed toward the summit. Hedges at the roadside hung heavy with elderberries and yew berries, hips and haws. Large clusters of birds eagerly partook of this final feast of the season.

Throughout their drive, Celia and Anthony shared a lively conversation. He asked about her sisters; she asked about his brother. They talked of the weather, the harvest. When they arrived at a gorse-covered knoll at the head of the valley, Anthony stopped the carriage and helped Celia to alight. After tying the horses, he offered his arm and they walked on, following a footpath that threaded its way along the lip of the knoll and allowed a sweeping vista of hills and vales below. Some of the trees had begun to change color, spattering the hillsides with dots of orange and yellow.

Anthony placed his free hand over Celia's where it lay on his arm. She glanced up at him.

"It's pleasant," he said, "having time alone like this."

Being reminded that they were, in fact, quite alone left Celia tongue-tied.

After a few moments Anthony spoke again. "I had a brief conversation with your mother this morning after breakfast. Did she tell you about it?"

"No. Should she have?"

He shrugged. "I thought she might have said something." He stopped and turned to face Celia, taking her hands in his. "I told her that as soon as I have returned you both to London, I intend to travel to Yorkshire to ask your father for your hand in marriage." As he looked down at her upturned face, he detected a hint of a smile mixed with pleased surprise. Taking her gently by the waist he pulled her to him, planting a warm kiss full upon her lips.

Experiencing her first kiss ever from a man, Celia felt her insides jump and flutter. The softness of his lips sent chills racing through her body to the very tips of her toes. Drawn by the strength she sensed behind the gentleness of his touch, she involuntarily leaned toward him, and he tightened his hold on her.

When he finally drew away, she kept her hands lying along his forearms, not willing to allow the glorious moment of intimacy to pass. As he smiled at her and spoke, she focused her eyes on the fine, sensual lips that had given her such pleasure.

There was a hint of laughter in his voice. "I suppose I may assume from your reaction that you would welcome my suit?"

"I should like it, sir, above all things."

"Until such time, then, as I can speak with your father, I shall consider us unofficially engaged. And it would please me if you would call me Anthony."

Some minutes later the couple retraced their steps to the carriage and began the return trip to Walsh Priory. Part of this journey was accomplished in companionable silence. Anthony was delighted that Celia had accepted him, for he was as certain as he could be that she was the perfect woman for him.

For her part Celia was having difficulty believing her own good fortune. She had previously permitted herself to dream—to hope. But this was no longer a dream. He had proposed! She had accepted. Her father's permission was the merest formality. How jealous all her London friends would be when they learned that she had attached the young, handsome, wealthy, and personable Mr. Graydon. She could hardly wait to see their reaction!

And then there was that one final glory that would be hers. The Earl of Walsh was not long for this world, she had seen that for herself. And though she wished him no ill, she truly felt that it would not be long before he traveled on to his final rest. When that happened, she—Celia Demming, youngest daughter of a Yorkshire wool empire— would be Celia Demming Graydon, Countess of Walsh.

Celia was interrupted from this glorious reverie

when Anthony slowed his horses to acknowledge a rider approaching from the opposite direction.

"Celia, here is someone you must meet." He uttered her name casually, as easily as if he had used it all his life.

Just hearing it thrilled her. It sounded so possessive. She struggled to focus her thoughts on the rider ahead. It was a young woman near Celia's own age, mounted on a handsome brown hack. The young lady's habit of dark blue wool was neither fashionable nor new, but it had been cut with skill and showed her slim figure to advantage. As she came closer, Celia could see that her dark hair had been braided and pinned up beneath her hat. Large brown eyes peered out from a comely, smiling face.

"Anthony," she said as she reined in her horse and Anthony stopped his pair. "Your mother told me you were home. Somehow I keep missing you."

She paused then, giving Anthony an opportunity to introduce his companion.

"I had been meaning to call on you. I would like you to meet Miss Celia Demming. She is staying at the Priory." As the two young women nodded and smiled, Anthony turned to Celia. "This is Miss Ursula Browne; her father is rector of Little Graydon."

"I am pleased to make your acquaintance, Miss Browne," Celia said. "I have heard Lady Walsh speak of you."

"She told me you have been stopping every day," Anthony added. "I want you to know how much I appreciate it."

Ursula shrugged this thank-you off as she said,

"Your mother is a saint. It is no trial to spend time with her. But I must say good-bye to you both, for I am late. I was due at the orphanage ten minutes ago. It was a pleasure to meet you, Miss Demming." Then, with only a nod, Ursula urged her horse past the carriage and into a canter as she hurried on her way.

"What a lovely young woman," Celia commented as Anthony set his horses in motion.

"Is she?" He seemed to consider for a moment before he said, "Yes. I suppose she is. I can't say that I ever noticed."

"Have you known her long?"

"Since she was eight or nine years old."

"Well, then, that explains it, doesn't it?"

"I suppose so."

"Should she be riding alone?" Celia asked, amazed that any young woman would be permitted to ride unescorted.

"She always does. She'll come to no harm. Besides, the rector doesn't employ a groom."

"Surely there is some stable lad who could go with her?"

"Probably. But I can't see Ursula having any patience with that. She's a headstrong girl, accustomed to having her own way."

Celia made no reply. Her mother had always insisted that headstrong girls were destined for self-destruction, and she couldn't conceive of what it must be like to "have one's own way."

That evening at dinner, Celia blushed becomingly when Anthony announced their unofficial engagement. Both Mrs. Demming and Lady Walsh voiced their approval and concurred that a spring wedding would be just the thing.

"It is our custom to have a house party for the shooting in November," Lady Walsh added, directing her remark at Mrs. Demming. "You and Celia must come. And Mr. Demming, too, should he care for it."

"What a kind invitation, Lady Walsh," Lavinia said, "but indeed we cannot accept. Two of my daughters are increasing, and I have promised to be with them during their confinements. Melinda is expecting her child in mid-November, and Sophia, soon after Christmas."

"Then you must allow Celia to come to us," Lady Walsh persisted. "She and Anthony would then have an opportunity to become better acquainted, and Celia could meet some of our friends and other members of the family."

Mrs. Demming did not commit herself to this plan, but later that evening when she and Celia were alone, she asked how Celia felt about the invitation.

"I should like to come. It's lovely here, and Lady Walsh is correct. I don't know Mr. Graydon—Anthony—all that well, and it would allow us more time together. If I go off to Yorkshire now, I probably won't see him again until the wedding. And another thing, Mama. It gets rather lonely for me at home now with everyone else gone."

"My only concern is that you should be properly chaperoned, Celia."

"Lady Walsh will be my chaperon, Mama. And

didn't she say her sister will be here, too? Then, there will be the wives of the gentlemen who are invited for the shooting."

"But what of Mr. Graydon, Celia? Will he hold the line with you?"

Celia didn't pretend to misunderstand. "He has been a perfect gentleman, Mama. Have you forgotten how wonderfully he behaved when I fell down the stairs? I will always be grateful to him for his delicacy on that occasion. I trust him completely, else I would not have agreed to wed him. But if you will allow me to come, I will be careful to remember all you taught me. I will guard against any situation that might be considered even the least bit compromising. I solemnly promise."

Celia held her breath while she waited for her mother's decision. The previous winter in Yorkshire had seemed to last forever. To spend even part of this winter in Buckinghamshire would be a wonderful reprieve.

"Very well," Lavinia said. "We will go back to London tomorrow as planned. Then, after Mr. Graydon has formally called upon your papa, and if your papa approves, we will permit you to accept Lady Walsh's invitation."

Celia smiled inwardly. Her mama had already made up her mind, and her papa always deferred to his wife in matters concerning their daughters.

Celia returned to London and allowed herself to be swept into the current of her social calendar while she waited for Anthony to visit Yorkshire. What few whispers still circulated concerning her tumble down the stairs were forgotten entirely when the announcement of her engagement to Anthony Graydon appeared simultaneously in the pages of both the *Post* and the *Gazette*.

When Anthony called to put the engagement ring on her finger, she cried. All the years of hard work: the French and deportment lessons, the hours of practice on the pianoforte, the endless fittings and hair dressings—all the sacrifice had paid dividends she had never anticipated. Her future now seemed brighter than she had imagined even in her most fantastic dreams. She had never been so happy in her life.

In the early days of November, Lavinia Demming headed west to settle herself into Melinda's home in Cornwall while Celia accepted her fiancé's escort to Walsh Priory. This time she had packed all the clothes she had with her in London and had taken her mother's maid as well. Lavinia insisted that no one could dress Celia's hair as Wylie could, and besides, she would not need Wylie while she sat about Cornwall waiting to become a grandmother for the fifth time. Celia and the maid occupied the coach while Anthony once again rode alongside. This caused Celia no small amount of concern, for the day was chill with a strong wind blowing.

"Surely you should ride inside with us," Celia suggested when she became aware of Anthony's plans.

"I won't be cold."

"But if it should start to rain, you could catch your death."

Her genuine concern for his health caused him to

smile indulgently at her. "If it should begin to rain, I promise you, I will come inside. Does that content you?"

She had agreed but still watched him anxiously whenever she caught a glimpse of him through the window. She and Wylie were warmly supplied with heated bricks at their feet and a thick fur rug over their legs.

Lady Walsh seemed to be watching for them, for no sooner had they entered the hall than she was there full of delightful news. On the previous day while she was sitting with her husband, he had turned his head to look at her and had recognized her.

"He looked right at me and said, 'Frances, is that you?' I was that flabbergasted I couldn't think what to say for a moment. Then, of course, I said it was me and how did he feel? He said he felt tired but wanted to know where you were, Anthony—and Robert. I told him you were in London, but expected today. Then I told him that Robert had gone with the army to deal with Bonaparte, and when he looked troubled, I said that we had soundly beaten Boney, and he was exiled forever. He seemed delighted at that, said I should send both you and Robert to him as soon as you arrived, and then he drifted off again. I wanted to tell him about your engagement, but I didn't have a chance. Today he doesn't know me again, but surely that was a good sign, don't you think?"

Both Anthony and Celia agreed that this was indeed wonderful news. Then, while Lady Walsh rattled on in much the same vein, Celia took her arm and walked with her to a sofa in the drawing room. Anthony directed the footmen to unload the baggage coach while the butler was sent for tea.

The drawing room was predominantly blue, quite large but made comfortably warm by a wood fire burning on the hearth. When Anthony moved toward the fire, Celia was convinced that he had been chilled by his ride. Lady Walsh had progressed into a discussion of her family. "My oldest sister died several years ago; she is the one who left her entire estate to Anthony."

This was news to Celia, but she pretended only polite interest.

"My younger sister, Mary, is arriving tomorrow. She is totally idle, but so good-natured one cannot help but like her. Our other guests don't arrive for several days, so you will have plenty of time to settle in."

Celia soon went upstairs to change for dinner. There she found Wylie directing two chambermaids in the unpacking of various trunks and portmanteau.

"What dress will you wear for dinner, Miss Celia?" Wylie asked as she folded delicate underthings and stowed them into a large oak chest near the wardrobe.

Celia opened her mouth to respond, then closed it again, feeling silly. She had no idea what she should wear. In fact, she realized with a sense of shock, that she had never been asked that question before. As Wylie repeated the question, Celia put her off with, "Let's dress my hair first. I'll decide on a gown later."

Since she had already finished washing, she sat down in her chemise on the bench before the dressing table and regarded herself in the mirror as Wylie removed pins and brushed out the burnished curls.

Celia suddenly felt cold and realized her hands were shaking. She gripped them together on the table to still them. Always self-assured and confident in the past, she was suddenly afraid. Wylie had asked a simple question; surely Celia could answer it. What should she wear? A quiet dinner in the country with only the countess, Anthony, and herself. What would be appropriate? She had dozens of dresses. Which would best suit the occasion?

She could wear the dark pink muslin—or was it too light for such a cool evening? The green wool, then—though it was rather simple for her first night at Walsh Priory. What would Lady Walsh wear, she wondered? She had no idea.

Was it really possible that in all her years of training she had not learned how to dress herself? It was true. She realized now that she had never once made a decision herself about what to wear, or how to dress her hair. Even her jewelry and accessories had been chosen by her mother.

Her hair was finished now, neatly arranged and shining. She rose from the bench and addressed Wylie with as much assurance as she could put into her voice. "I don't know what I feel like wearing tonight, Wylie. Why don't you pick something from those things that are already unpacked?"

Trained never to question an order, Wylie responded, "Very good, miss. The blue velvet is here. It is simple and flattering."

"That will be fine, Wylie, thank you." Celia stepped into the dress and allowed herself to be buttoned up. She collected the accessories she had used the last time she wore it and made her way downstairs, but the confidence she had felt earlier in the day had been soundly shaken.

When she arrived in the drawing room, Anthony and the countess had already returned. Anthony was elegant in a dark coat with pristine lace at the throat and wrists. Celia smiled at him then went to sit near his mother. She listened while Lady Walsh enumerated some of the entertainments she had planned for her female guests while the men were out "slaughtering birds."

"Then in the evening when the gentlemen are with us, sometimes we play at charades. Always great fun. Ursula Browne is especially good at them. You met her, I believe, when you were here last."

"Yes, briefly."

"You must get to know her better. She is a delightful girl, so good-hearted and generous. I often invite her when we have company; there is so little entertainment for her otherwise."

"Does she never go to London?"

"I don't believe so. Hers is a family of modest means."

"She also says she has no use for the ton," Anthony added. "Considers London's social whirl a waste of both money and time."

42

Celia decided that Ursula Browne was a fool. She was a handsome girl, but she would never be noticed tucked away in the Chiltern Hills. Lavinia was fond of saying that wares collecting dust on the back of the shelf would never catch the buyer's eye. Beautiful things had to be dusted off and pushed to the forefront where they could be noticed, appreciated, and acquired.

Somewhere in the house a door slammed. Distant muffled voices grew louder and soon a disturbance moved close to the drawing room doors. Celia turned her head with curiosity. When a voice was raised in exclamation, Anthony stood. He had taken only one step toward the door when it was flung open and the butler stood there.

"What is it, Leech?" Anthony asked, clearly annoyed at the butler's indecorous behavior.

"Excuse me, sir, but it's a miracle!" This burst of excited speech from a man who never raised his voice and routinely responded in a monotone, brought Lady Walsh to her feet.

When Leech moved away from the door, Celia observed two men making rather slow progress across the wide marble floor of the great hall. As they entered the drawing room, they stepped from the relative darkness of the hall into the circle of light from a candelabra on a table near the door.

"God be praised!" Lady Walsh whispered weakly as she swayed. Celia moved quickly to steady her.

At exactly the same moment as the countess spoke, Anthony cried, "Robert! I knew you were alive! I knew it!" He crossed the room in a few quick strides and enveloped his brother in an embrace.

Chapter 4

LADY WALSH APPEARED to be struck dumb. Celia stood beside her, supporting her and staring in disbelief herself at the apparition that Anthony was greeting with such joy. She could not doubt that this was Robert, Viscount Wexford, but she was staggered by his appearance. He was tall, as tall as Anthony, but appeared much thinner. His fair hair was long and unkempt, much of his face obscured by a thick growth of beard. He appeared to be wearing peasants' clothing: brown trousers and a loose shirt of cheap, coarse cloth. The trousers were too short, ending above his ankles and exposing a pair of shabby farmers' boots. His blue wool coat was out at the elbows and none too clean. The young man who stood beside him, supporting him, was dressed in similar fashion.

Wexford blinked, then smiled, when his brother embraced him. Celia noticed that he did not look at Anthony, however, nor did he seem to notice his mother a few yards away. His eyes were bright blue and piercing, but they seemed to focus on some distant space.

"Tony," he said, his voice warm with emotion, "it's

45

so good to be home. I have much to tell you, but first you must meet Pierre Amay. I owe him my life."

Pierre seemed taken aback when Anthony extended a hand to him, but he offered his own and Anthony shook it vigorously. "You have my gratitude, sir, and that of my entire family."

"I'm afraid he doesn't have much English, Tony," Wexford said.

Anthony repeated his words in French. Pierre nodded and smiled but said nothing.

Anthony took his brother's free arm. "What happened to you? What is the injury to your leg? Where have you been all these months?"

Wexford smiled at this barrage of questions as he limped forward. "Whoa, there! All of your questions will be answered, but first things first. How is Father?"

"Much the same as he was when you left, though he asked after you just yesterday."

"And where is Mother?"

Anthony stopped walking and swung around to gaze at his brother. Celia watched as his first puzzled frown resolved into a look of alarm.

Lady Walsh, who in the first moments of the brothers' reunion had remained silent, now stepped toward her elder son with her arms outstretched. "I am here, Robert. You can't see me." It was a statement, not a question.

He embraced her, then bent to kiss her cheek. "No, Mother, I'm afraid not."

As Lady Walsh's eyes filled with tears, Celia took

her arm and led her to a chair while Anthony helped his brother to a couch near the fire.

"Don't despair, though," Wexford added, his voice hopeful. "I saw a doctor in London earlier today who is supposed to know what he's talking about. He says there's a good chance that my sight will return."

"But I don't understand," Lady Walsh said. "Why didn't you write to us, let us know that you were alive?"

"I couldn't. I'd had this ghastly blow to the head. I was unconscious for days. When I did wake up, not only couldn't I see, but I hadn't the least notion who I was. As time went by, little pieces of memory came back slowly. Then one morning just four days ago, when I woke up I knew my name, remembered where I lived. I suspected I could get here as fast as any letter could, probably faster. So I asked Pierre to bring me, and here we are. Which reminds me. There is a coach outside waiting to be paid."

While Anthony rang for the butler and sent him to pay the coachman, Wexford continued, "Pierre and I financed our entire journey on the proceeds of that signet ring I was so fond of. It was the only thing of value that I had. Fortunately, the money lasted until we reached London."

"Did you stop at the house?"

"Only long enough to find it closed and not a single coach team in the stables. I can't imagine what convinced the coachman we hired to bring us here without pay, for I don't think he believed me when I told him who I was."

"Robert," Anthony said, "there is someone else

47

here in the room that I should very much like you to meet."

Celia had tried to remain discreetly in the background, feeling like an intruder during this dramatic family reunion, but as Anthony held out his hand to her, she came forward to join him.

"I've become engaged while you've been gone," Anthony said. "This is my fiancée, Miss Celia Demming."

Wexford's eyes widened in surprise and, Celia thought, pleasure as well. "You cunning devil!" he remarked to his brother. "Congratulations!"

As he started to rise unsteadily to his feet, Celia said, "Please, Lord Wexford, don't stand. You're not well." Now that she was closer, she decided that he looked very ill indeed. His face was extremely thin, and his complexion held a sickly pallor. There were dark circles beneath his eyes.

Ignoring her protests, he stood awkwardly and extended one hand. She placed her own in it.

"I am delighted to make your acquaintance, ma'am. I must apologize for my appearance. I am in no proper state for my mother's drawing room, and well I know it. I know you all have questions, and I promise to answer them, but right now I am longing for a bath."

"And you shall have one," Anthony agreed. "With your permission, Mother, I will have Leech put dinner back one hour. Will that give you enough time, Robert?"

"It should. Mother, if you will excuse me, I will return as soon as I may. It was a pleasure to meet you, Miss Demming."

"And you, my lord," she replied as the brothers left the room together, closely followed by the silent Pierre.

Lady Walsh watched her sons until they disappeared into the great hall. Then she turned to Celia. "I have prayed unceasingly for the safe return of my son. Today those prayers have been answered. I should like to go to church, my dear. Will you come with me?"

"Certainly, Lady Walsh, I shall be happy to."

A message was sent round to the stables for a closed carriage, while a maid hurried to fetch the ladies' cloaks. The coach collected them within fifteen minutes and shortly thereafter deposited them at the Little Graydon church.

The nave of the church was dark and cold, but the pale light of the evening sky passing through the high windows allowed sufficient light for Lady Walsh to make her way toward the front of the sanctuary. Celia let her go alone while she herself sat in a back pew.

It was only then, in the quiet church, that the whole picture presented itself to Celia. Anthony and Lady Walsh were filled with thankfulness that their dear Robert had been restored to them. But Celia's future was no longer so rosy, for with the return of Viscount Wexford her chance of ever becoming the Countess of Walsh had become an extremely remote possibility.

Celia and Lady Walsh had returned from church and were waiting in the drawing room when the men came downstairs nearly an hour later. A bath and a change of clothing had done much to restore Lord Wexford to the semblance of a gentleman. His dark blond hair had been washed and brushed back from his high forehead. His face was clean-shaven. Celia noted that even though his coat was well cut and in the first stare of fashion, it hung loosely from his shoulders. He had shifted the weight of his bad leg to a walking stick, and held Anthony's arm in a casual way, allowing himself to be guided around obstacles of furniture as if he had been unsighted all his life.

Celia felt great pity for him. What if the doctor was wrong and his sight never returned? How tragic that would be.

"Your friend Pierre is not joining us, my lord?" Celia asked as they made their way into the dining room.

Wexford's eyes narrowed as he turned his head toward the sound of her voice. "No. Tony tried to persuade him, but he insisted he would be more comfortable eating in the kitchen. Perhaps he is right. Considering that his home has only two rooms, it is understandable that he would find this heap intimidating."

Earlier, while Wexford had bathed and changed, Anthony had withheld his questions, knowing that the others would wish to hear all his brother had to say. Now, as the butler served soup to the ladies, he could no longer contain his curiosity.

"How did you meet Pierre?"

"He was in the Dutch-Belgian army, and his wife was helping to tend the wounded at a field hospital."

"If you were taken to hospital, why is it that I couldn't find you?"

"Patience, Tony. It is a complicated story, and I'm not even certain I have it all untangled. But I can tell you what conclusions I have drawn from the facts I have been able to piece together."

Leech carefully placed a bowl of soup before Wexford as he said very quietly, "Your soup, my lord. The spoon is on the right."

Celia, sitting directly across from Wexford, watched as he moved his fingers cautiously across the table until he encountered the spoon handle. He picked it up. With his left hand, he felt carefully for the edge of the bowl, then slowly ladled a spoonful and brought it to his lips. She looked away, ashamed of herself for staring. After a few moments he put down the spoon and spoke again.

"I'm sure you've heard the details of the battle by now. I was involved for most of the day. I'd had a few minor wounds, nothing that slowed me down much. I don't remember being hit, or even where I was at the time. I must have been near part of the Dutch-Belgian contingent, however, because I ended up in one of their hospitals. Pierre's wife was working there. Since my uniform had been cut away, and I was covered with a Belgian army blanket, she assumed I was part of their army. I was unconscious for days. When I finally woke up, I couldn't see, I couldn't talk, and I didn't know who I was."

Lady Walsh's eyes once again filled with tears, and her hand reached to cover his where it lay on the table beside his soup bowl.

When he felt her fingers touch him, he turned his hand over and took hers in a reassuring clasp. He turned his head toward her and smiled. "It's all right, Mother. I know what you're thinking. And you're right. It was awful. Most of the people around me were speaking French, and for a while I think I thought I was French. But all of the thoughts in my head were in English, so I was confused. I couldn't understand where I was or why. Then I started to remember the battle . . . and I wished for a long time that I had died there. I was so close to dead anyway, surely oblivion would have been better than the confusion, the darkness, and the pain."

Wexford carefully inched his hand toward his wineglass. Anthony picked it up and said, "Here it is," and placed it in his brother's hand.

Wexford took a generous swallow, then set the glass down cautiously. "When both my head and leg wounds had healed enough for me to leave the hospital, they didn't know what to do with me. Most of the wounded had family or friends who would come to claim them, but they didn't know where I belonged. Pierre was a volunteer and had already been discharged, so he and Marie took me home with them to a little cottage east of Louvain. They have next to nothing, but they shared all with me."

He paused and began slowly to spoon his soup. When he finished, the butler removed the bowl and replaced it with a slice of guinea fowl.

"As the days passed, and I sat outside the cottage in the sun and listened to the birds and the sounds of summer, memories started to come back to me, slowly at first and then more quickly. I remembered the battle, the faces of my fellow officers and the men in my command. I saw their uniforms, and finally I remembered their names. Then I knew for certain that I was English. I remembered fishing in the Thames as a boy; I remembered attending Oxford. As the concussion or whatever it was healed, my speech returned. The first words I said were in English, and Pierre and Marie were astonished. They wanted to go immediately to the British authorities in Brussels, but I asked them to wait, and they agreed.

"It was bizarre discovering myself and my life bit by bit, day after day. I remembered your face, Mother, and Father's, and Tony's—and your names, too, before I remembered my own."

Anthony, seeing his brother's plate untouched, said, "If you don't care for the fowl, is there something else you would like?"

"No, thank you. I'm not hungry."

"You must eat, Robert," Lady Walsh stated. "How else will you regain your strength?"

As he turned to his mother and smiled once again, Celia watched his eyes. She felt they mirrored the frustration of their owner. She saw indulgence for his mother's solicitude, but she also saw sadness, impatience, and above all, weariness—not only in his eyes, but in his whole face, the movements of his hands, the sagging of his shoulders. She suspected he was still in considerable physical pain.

"I think you look exceedingly weary, Lord Wexford," Celia commented. "And I believe we have tired you."

"I must admit, Miss Demming, that I desire nothing so much as my bed."

"Then to bed you will go, and straightaway," Anthony said, rising from the table and waiting to take Robert's arm.

"I will look in on Father when I go upstairs," Wexford said, "and I will see you ladies tomorrow."

As the gentlemen left the room, Celia reflected on how tragic a simple statement like "I'll see you tomorrow" could be, when uttered by someone who had lost the gift of sight.

"He is so thin," Lady Walsh said mournfully, "and he ate nothing."

"We must remember, my lady, that he is no longer accustomed to rich foods," Celia said. "He will need time to adjust. And remember, too, that it is difficult to eat without sight. Perhaps if you—" She broke off suddenly, afraid she was being presumptuous.

"Perhaps what, my dear? What was it you were about to say?"

"It's really not my place, Lady Walsh."

"Nonsense, child. If you have a suggestion that may help Wexford, please share it with me, for I have no experience with such a situation."

"I thought that perhaps you could have your cook send up some cold things for Lord Wexford. Perhaps some cold meat that he could eat with his fingers, without an audience."

Lady Walsh frowned at the thought of anyone eating such food with their fingers, but had to admit that Celia's words made sense. "Why don't you speak to Cook for me, dear. I suspect you will know much better than I what would be appropriate. And if you will excuse me, I believe I will retire. I know it's early, but the day has been eventful."

"I think that's an excellent idea, my lady. I am tired myself, and thought perhaps I would take a book to bed after I have bid Anthony good night."

Upstairs, Celia waited for Anthony outside Wexford's rooms, which were directly across the corridor from her own. When he joined her there, she said, "Your mother has gone to bed, and I'm going, too. I wanted to say good night first."

He took her hands, and she smiled at him. "I can't begin to tell you how happy I am," he said.

"You don't need to. I can see it in your face."

"These last months have been hell, not wanting to believe he was dead, but with each day and week that passed, fearing the worst. I'm so relieved." He laughed lightheartedly. "I feel so unburdened, so light, as if I could fly." Then suddenly his voice and his eyes grew serious. "Between finding you, Celia, and having Robert come home, I believe I am the luckiest man in the world."

After Anthony left his brother's room, Lord Wexford's valet helped him to undress and prepare for bed. Wanting to be alone, Wexford soon dismissed the man. "You need not come in the morning until I ring, Gregson."

"Very good, my lord. I have set the fire screen.

There are three candles burning by the bed. And may I say it's good to have you back, sir."

"Thank you, Gregson. It's good to be back, and I will remember the candles. Good night."

"Good night, my lord."

Wexford moved toward his bed, sat down on its edge, and sighed. The reunion with his family had taken what little strength he had remaining after the strain of the journey home from Belgium. He was weary to his bones.

There was a quiet knock at the door. Annoyed, he bid the knocker to enter.

"I have brought you up a tray, my lord, from the kitchen."

The voice was that of the butler; Wexford motioned him into the room.

"Do I see my mother's hand in this, Leech?"

"No, my lord. It was Miss Demming who asked me to speak with Cook."

"Indeed?"

"Yes, my lord. She has ordered cold chicken, bread, and cheese. She said she felt these things would be more like those you are presently accustomed to. There is also a glass of . . . a glass of . . ."

"Have you suddenly developed a stammer, Leech? A glass of what?"

"Milk, my lord."

"Milk?"

"Yes, my lord."

"And pray what am I to do with that?"

"I believe she wishes you to drink it, my lord, for she said she felt it would do you much more good than wine on an empty stomach."

"I expect she may be right about that. Give it to me."

With wide-eyed, openmouthed disbelief, which unfortunately the viscount was not able to appreciate, Leech put the brimming glass into Wexford's hand, then stared in astonishment as the viscount tipped the glass and drained it to the bottom.

Wexford instructed the butler to leave the tray and then dismissed him. After Leech had gone, he made a fair meal of the "finger food" Miss Demming had thoughtfully provided for him.

Chapter 5

CELIA WOKE VERY early the following morning. She had spent a restless night, disturbed by the momentous events of the previous evening. Knowing she would sleep no more, she rose, dressed carefully in a simple gray morning gown, and went downstairs. The house was quiet. Only the servants were about, cleaning the grates and laying new fires.

She went into the salon where a large fire already warmed the room comfortably. The draperies had been pulled aside from several sets of french doors that faced toward the east. A thin mist lay over the gray-green parkland that rolled away beyond the windows. Orange and yellow leaves drifted down from the trees to settle in thick layers on the carefully scythed grass. Celia opened one of the doors a crack to breathe the sweet autumn air.

The sound of voices speaking French came to her. To her left where the carriage drive met the great front portico, a coach had pulled up before the house. Lord Wexford and his Belgian friend stood beside it, engaged in conversation.

"You are up very early," Anthony's voice came

from behind her. She turned her head to smile at him, but stayed by the windows as he crossed the room to her.

"I retired early," she said. "It's a beautiful morning."

"When this mist burns off, we should have a bright day."

"It appears as if Pierre is leaving," she said. "Will you have the doctor attend your brother?"

"I have already sent for him, though Robert won't be pleased."

"My mother says that we don't always like what is best for us."

"What sage advice," Anthony answered. "If Robert objects too strenuously, I shall impart your mother's words to him."

Celia watched as the two men outside shook hands, then Pierre entered the coach and it started off down the drive, passing before the doors where she and Anthony stood.

"I believe your brother grew quite attached to Pierre during the time they spent together."

"I think you're right. Wait for me. I'll tell him we are here."

As Anthony left the room, Wexford continued to stand in the drive until the sound of the coach faded away. When he turned, Celia saw that he had the ebony walking stick in his hand. He used this to feel his way to the bottom of the wide stairway rising to the front door. As he ascended the stairs, he disappeared from her view.

A few minutes later the brothers crossed the hall together; Anthony was speaking. "Aunt Mary is arriving today. There is no way I can forestall her. But we shall send word to the others and put them off."

"Don't be ridiculous, Tony. There's no reason to cancel because of me. Let our friends come. Let them enjoy themselves."

As the men entered the salon, Anthony said, "Here is Celia."

"Good morning, Miss Demming," Wexford said. "What do you think of Tony's plan to put off his shooting party?"

"I think he should do whatever will make you most comfortable, my lord. You are not fully recovered from your wounds, and you need rest."

"Having people to stay will not keep me from resting. I want you to proceed with your plans, Tony. But please don't include me in them. I'm not yet eager for company."

Anthony and Celia exchanged glances, and when she nodded at him, he said, "All right, we will let them come."

When Wexford returned upstairs, Celia and Anthony adjourned to the breakfast parlor. Afterward, when Anthony was called away to meet with his father's gamekeeper and Lady Walsh went to sit with her husband, Celia found herself with nothing to do.

If she were in London, she would be at home to a string of morning callers, or go shopping in Bond Street, or study fashion plates and endure endless dress fittings. Even in the country she had a daily regimen prescribed by her mother: French and Italian lessons in the morning, practice on the piano-forte, calls to the neighbors, daily meetings with the housekeeper during which she was to listen intently while her mother held forth on housekeeping concerns, upcoming menus, and future dinner parties.

She made her way to the drawing room where the pianoforte sat. It was an excellent instrument, finer than the one she played at her own home.

Nearly an hour later, tired of this occupation, she decided to find Lady Walsh and ask if there was some needlework she could do. Perhaps there were some handkerchiefs to monogram. She knew she would very much enjoy doing such a task for Anthony. As she walked through the great hall, she collected the London papers that had arrived with the morning post. If Lady Walsh had no work for her, she would take them to the morning room and occupy herself with society news.

On her way to the stairway she passed near the study door, which was slightly ajar. She heard Lord Wexford's voice raised in exasperation, "For God's sake, Leech, will you stop hovering over me! I am not an infant! Go away. And don't come back unless I ring for you."

Celia could hear no answer from the chastised servant, but she could clearly hear his footsteps approaching the door. She paused in the hallway as Leech exited the room and closed the door quietly.

"Good morning, miss," he said as he noticed her.

Embarrassed for having overheard, Celia said, "I'm sure he doesn't mean to be short with you,

Leech, but it must be difficult for him, not being able to see. And he is still in pain from his wounds."

"Of course, miss. Is there anything I can get you?"

"No, thank you, Leech. I was just passing by."

"Very good, miss." The butler then bowed briefly and walked away.

Celia continued on her way for a few steps and then stopped suddenly. No doubt Lord Wexford was as bored as she was. Perhaps he would like her to read to him. She had the latest papers in her hand. All the London news he had not heard for months. She stepped back to the study door and knocked.

Wexford's gruff, "Who is it?" did not dismay her, for she knew he was out of sorts, angry at his butler.

"It is Miss Demming, my lord."

There was a silence of perhaps ten seconds before he gave permission for her to enter. She opened the door briskly and left it standing wide as she entered the room. Lord Wexford stood before a large chair near the fire. In front of the chair sat a footstool, and beside it on the floor lay a quilted lap rug.

Impatient with his strict adherence to the rules of etiquette, she said, "You must not leap to your feet, sir, only because custom requires it. How will your leg heal if you do not have a care for it? Please, sit down."

As he reseated himself and leaned forward to lift

his leg back to the stool, she picked up the lap rug and rearranged it.

"Has Tony left you on your own?" he asked.

"He has gone off to be sure all the birds are as they should be for your guests," she said, seating herself near him.

"And my mother?"

"She is with Lord Walsh."

"Does she spend much time with him?"

"Yes, she does. She talks to him, tells him about her day, about you and Anthony, the neighbors and so forth. She is convinced he understands her. And perhaps she is right, for he recognized her a few days ago."

"Did you want something specifically from me, Miss Demming?"

"Yes, indeed. I have brought the London papers. I thought I could make myself useful by reading to you. What should you like to hear?"

She had been unfolding the paper, but when he didn't answer, she glanced up at him. He had grown quite still, gazing intently in her direction.

"Why did you really come in?"

"I was passing the door, and I heard what you said to Leech."

"You think I was harsh with him."

"It is not my place to comment on your behavior, my lord."

"I would appreciate your opinion, nevertheless, Miss Demming."

"My mother has taught me that I should never offer any opinion on the behavior of gentlemen."

"In general, I would consider that excellent advice," he said. "I would, however, in this instance welcome your comments as a relatively objective observer."

After a few moments' pause, Celia answered carefully. "I think Leech is devoted to you and concerned for your comfort and well-being. I also think that if you are angry and wish to snap at someone, it should be at Anthony, or even me, rather than the servants. We won't take it as personally as they do."

"And what makes you think I am angry?"

"It's just a feeling I had last night, while you were relating your experiences of the past few months. I had the impression you were leaving the most important things unsaid."

She paused then and waited for his reply, but the moments lengthened uncomfortably before he finally answered. "If you will excuse me, Miss Demming, I would appreciate, as I told Leech, being left alone."

Celia felt as if she had been slapped in the face and was grateful that Lord Wexford could not see the blush she could feel burning on her cheeks. She rose to her feet, folded the papers, and laid them on the chair where she had been sitting. Then, without a word, she left the room.

Satisfied that the Priory's birds were present in sufficient quantity to supply his guests with good sport, Anthony turned back toward the main house in the early afternoon. The mist of the morning had indeed burned off, and the day was fine. At the crossroads where the road into Little Graydon intersected the pike road to High Wycombe, he encountered Ursula Browne on her way to the Priory to visit with his mother. They rode together through the crisp November sunshine.

"When did you get back?" she asked.

"Yesterday. Have you heard the news?"

She smiled. "Yes. Your mother told Father when she came to church last night. It was all over the village in no time. You were right all along, Tony. You said he was alive. I wanted to come last night, but I knew you all needed some time alone."

"Do you know about his eyes?"

"Yes. But Lady Walsh said there is hope, so we must pray. Do you think he will see me . . . I mean . . . will he let me see him?"

"I honestly don't know. He is insisting that we go ahead with the house party, but has asked to be excluded."

"Who is coming this year?"

"My aunt Mary. She arrives this evening. My cousin John Hardy, Todd and Emily Crowther, Lord and Lady Matlock, Trevor Farr, Miss Demming, and of course, you."

"Miss Demming? The young lady you were driving with in the hills last month?"

"Yes. Miss Demming and I are engaged to be married."

"Engaged?" she said, her voice full of disbelief. "But I thought you met her only a few weeks ago?"

"We met in September. I asked her to marry me that day we saw you on the road, but we didn't announce the engagement until last week."

Ursula pulled her horse to a standstill, and Anthony was forced to do likewise.

"But, Tony, how can you marry someone you barely know?"

"I know her well enough to know that she is the perfect woman for me."

Ursula shook her head, a puzzled frown on her face. "I don't understand."

"You will, when you fall in love yourself someday."

She didn't answer him but nudged her horse into a trot. They covered the remaining distance to the Priory in silence.

When Viscount Wexford had dismissed Celia (for how else could she view his words save as a dismissal), she returned to the drawing room. There she sat gazing into the fire and marveling at her own stupidity.

It was true that during dinner the previous evening, she'd had a strong impression that Wexford's behavior, his very conversation, was stilted and unnatural. But whatever made her think she could say as much to his face? She didn't even know him. They were strangers. She had made the mistake of thinking that he was as forthright as Anthony. Clearly he did not appreciate it when people spoke honestly, from the heart.

She wanted above all things to be well-accepted by Anthony's family, for she suspected how uncomfortable life would be for one who was treated as an outsider. Now she had offended Lord Wexford, leading him to believe she was an impudent meddler.

Then she sighed as she realized she *was* an impudent meddler. She just couldn't understand when she had become one.

Celia had never cultivated the science of introspection. She had always taken one day at a time, doing without question everything that her father and mother, her governess, and even her sisters asked of her. She had discovered early on that life was easiest when one was obedient. No one ever shouted or became cross, or if they did, the tempest passed quickly for the error or transgression was accidental, not willful.

She seldom concerned herself with what motivated the people around her. She filled her days with doing what she was told, and if on a rare occasion someone did ask for her opinion, she generally deferred to others.

Now she suddenly discovered that in her new role, affianced to a man of means, she had powers she had never before exercised. It was time for her to stand on her own, function as an independent person; but she was not at all convinced that she had the necessary qualities to fill this rather large and unaccustomed role.

Celia rose to her feet with determination. She would go immediately to Lord Wexford and beg his pardon, even if it meant receiving another snub from him. Then, in future, if she should happen to be in his company, she would remember her mother's advice and keep her opinions to herself.

She exited the drawing room and knocked firmly on the study door. There was no answer. When she saw Leech crossing the great hall, she asked if he knew where Lord Wexford was at present.

"He has gone upstairs, miss, with the doctor, who arrived a few moments ago."

Before he had finished talking, the front door opened and Anthony and Ursula entered. Anthony smiled and greeted Celia, then said, "You remember Ursula Browne, do you not?"

"Yes, of course," Celia replied. "How do you do, Miss Browne."

"Is that Dr. Harrel's gig in the stable yard, Leech?" Anthony asked.

"Indeed, it is, sir."

"If you ladies will excuse me," Anthony said, "I should like to go upstairs to hear what the doctor has to say."

When Anthony turned toward the stairs, Celia smiled at Ursula. "Should you like to wait with me in the salon, Miss Browne, until Anthony returns?"

As they walked across the hall, Ursula said, "Anthony told me of your engagement, Miss Demming. Allow me to congratulate you. You are a very fortunate woman."

"Thank you, Miss Browne. And I agree; I am fortunate, indeed."

Remembering her conversational blunder with Wexford earlier in the day, Celia spoke with the greatest care. Ursula was eager for details of Lord Wexford's disappearance, and Celia shared these with her in the most general fashion. She related how the viscount had been wounded, how he had suffered temporary memory loss and been befriended by a Belgian soldier and his wife.

"The battle at Waterloo has been devastating for the estate," Ursula said. "Besides the injury to Lord Wexford, young Ned Forbes has lost a leg, and Mrs. Drew has been widowed."

"What will they do?"

"Mrs. Drew has a young son, and I don't see how she will be able to keep up the farm without her husband. I thought perhaps she could move to a cottage in the village, and we could find a place for her boy in the quarry. I intend to speak with Wexford about it, when he is better."

"What about the poor man who lost his leg?"

"He comes from a large family, and they are managing to get by. His mother sews well, and I have been bringing her some piecework." She looked at Celia expectantly. "Perhaps you might have something for her, Miss Demming. I assure you her work is excellent."

Celia smiled. She was warmed by the way Ursula's manner seemed to automatically include her in the concerns of the estate. She thought ruefully of how she had sought needlework for herself that very morning, but she said, "I will see what I can find for her. And I will speak to Lady Walsh, too . . . unless you have already done so."

"No. I try not to trouble her ladyship with other worries. She has enough to deal with in looking after Lord Walsh."

"Perhaps I could help in some way," Celia heard herself offering. "I have little experience, but I learn quickly."

"I go to the orphanage each Monday and Friday,"

Ursula offered. "You could come with me tomorrow if you like."

"What do you do there? I have always heard that orphanages are cold, strict, inhospitable places."

"Some are. The government takes no responsibility for orphans, so each community must deal in its own way. I believe in the cities most orphans end up in workhouses. My father established the orphanage shortly after he came to Little Graydon nearly twelve years ago. We solicit contributions from the property owners in the district, and the children all help—in the garden and with chores.

"And as for what I do there—I do whatever comes to hand. Sometimes the children need tutoring. Father insists they all be taught their letters, even though it is an unpopular policy in the village. Some of the older girls are learning to sew. Often a group of us will go for long walks. We watch the birds, or sail homemade boats on the pond. Occasionally we walk to the village for sweets. There are times when the young ones like to have a story read to them. Other times they only need someone to show compassion for a scraped knee."

It was nearly twenty minutes before Anthony joined them. They were by that time deep into a discussion of the orphanage. When he entered the room, they both looked up expectantly.

"What did the doctor say?" Celia asked.

"Much what I suspected. There is still healing to be done, but he believes that aside from some nasty scarring, the leg will someday be good as new. He would offer no opinion on the eyes, saying it was beyond his skills to predict."

"The expert in London offers hope," Ursula said, "and that is the prognosis we will believe." She rose from her chair. "I must be going now. Let me say again, Miss Demming, and to you, too, Anthony, that I wish you both happy."

After arranging to collect Celia the following day at two o'clock to take her along to the orphanage, Ursula declined Anthony's escort to the stables and left the house alone.

"What a remarkable young woman," Celia said after Ursula had gone.

"In what way remarkable?" Anthony asked.

"Many of the young women I know, including my own sisters, are supremely self-absorbed, spending all their time, all their energies on themselves. Ursula seems to think only of the well-being of others: the children at the orphanage, the tenants, your mother and father, even your brother. She is a truly good person."

"I suppose you're right. She's always the first one to lend a hand when someone needs help. Are you quite sure you wish to get involved in her projects?"

"Yes, I am sure. That is, if you have no objection?"

"I don't mind in the least."

"I'm pleased, because as lovely as it is to be here, I did find myself with time on my hands this morning."

"That will soon change. When our guests begin to arrive, you will have much to occupy you. As far as this afternoon is concerned, I have it all planned." He took her hand and drew her from her chair. "Come along. We are going to fetch a pelisse for you. I have ordered the curricle to be at the door in fifteen minutes."

"Where are we going?"

"I want to show you the house where we'll live, after we're married." These words were uttered quietly but with great intensity. The intimate nature of his words, combined with the passionate warmth in his eyes, made Celia blush.

Before she could think of anything to say, he drew her into his arms, holding her slight frame close against his tall one. "I know I should resist the temptation to tease you, but I find your blushes delightful, my dear Celia."

He bent his head and placed a gentle kiss upon her willing lips. "Once you have toured the house," he continued, "it will be easier for you to imagine us there together. Then, perhaps, you will be put to the blush less often."

He pulled her arm through his and guided her into the great hall. "We must hurry; we should not keep the horses standing overlong."

Seated comfortably in Anthony's curricle, racing along behind a well-behaved pair of glossy chestnuts, Celia and Tony traveled in a westerly direction for nearly an hour. Eventually they turned off the post road onto a beautifully curving drive through a heavy beech wood. They emerged from the woods into a clearing of carefully scythed lawn. Across this expanse of green, backed against a wood aflame with fall color, stood Merton Hall, a three-story structure of mellow red brick.

A large house by most standards, the Hall was small in comparison to the vastness of Walsh Priory. This fact alone made Celia's first view of her future home appealing. Nevertheless, the knowledge that she would soon be mistress of this great establishment was intimidating, for though her mother had taught her well, she knew that there was an immense gulf between instruction in housekeeping and the actual job itself.

As they pulled to a stop before the house, she said earnestly, "I want more than anything to make a proper home for you, Anthony, but I'm not . . . I've never . . ." She broke off, not certain how to continue without sounding foolish.

As a groom jogged up to take the horses' heads, Anthony took her hand in his. "I know you've never done it before. I've never been a husband before. Why can't we learn as we go? It will be an adventure."

His smile was so infectious, Celia found herself smiling, too. And as she smiled, her heart lightened, for she knew Tony meant every word. She suspected that he had a sweetness of nature uncommon in men, and she felt prodigiously lucky to have linked her future to his.

Chapter 6

WHEN CELIA AND Anthony arrived back at the Priory, they discovered that Lady Walsh's sister had arrived. They found her supervising the disposition of her copious baggage in the front hall.

"That trunk goes to my room, but this square parcel—be gentle with it, young man! It contains delicate porcelain: a gift for Lady Walsh. If you jostle it so, it will be nothing but a heap of shards fit only for the dustbin."

At that moment she noticed Tony and his companion. She turned her back on the half-dozen or so footmen awaiting her instructions and hurried to her nephew with both hands outstretched. "My dearest Tony. How good it is to see you and how wonderful you look! And can this be Miss Demming, of whom your mother has written so much?"

"Indeed, Aunt, allow me to introduce Miss Celia Demming. Celia, this is my aunt Mary, the Viscountess Aylesbury."

As Celia rose from her curtsy, Lady Aylesbury took her hand and patted it enthusiastically. "You are lovely, my dear, simply lovely. I so look forward to becoming acquainted. But tell me, both of you. Is it true—this news that Leech has shared with me? Has Robert indeed come home?"

While Anthony took his aunt into the salon to relay to her the details of his brother's return, Celia went upstairs to change for dinner. It was early, and after her long, cold drive she was hoping to take time for a bath.

When she arrived at her room, Wylie had a message for her from Lord Wexford. "His lordship sent his man to ask if you could spare a moment when you returned from your drive, Miss Celia."

"Did he say what his lordship wanted?"

"No, miss. Only that he wishes to speak with you, if it is convenient."

"Where might I find him, Wylie?"

"He said he would be in the book room, miss. On this floor, first door to the right in the west wing."

"Very well. I'll go now. I should like a bath before dinner, Wylie."

"I'll see to having the water carried up directly, Miss Celia."

Celia left her room and moved toward the west wing with some trepidation. Her last meeting with Lord Wexford had not been a pleasant one. She couldn't imagine why he would want to speak with her, but she decided that she would take the opportunity to make the apology she had wished to make earlier.

She knocked firmly and was told to enter. She stopped inside the door. The room was dark-paneled with a plush carpet on the floor. It reminded her forcibly of her father's book room at her home in Yorkshire.

A huge desk stood to her right, the wall behind it covered from floor to ceiling with bookshelves. To her left several comfortable-looking chairs stood before the hearth where a large fire blazed. The dark blue velvet draperies were drawn tightly closed against the chill November evening, keeping the room deliciously warm.

Wexford rose from one of the chairs before the fire and turned to face the door. "Is that you, Miss Demming?"

"Yes, my lord."

"Won't you please come in?"

As she hesitated by the door, wondering whether to close it for privacy or leave it open for propriety, he said, "Close the door, if you would. I should like to hold the heat."

As the door clicked shut, he said, "Please, come and sit here by me, Miss Demming. I know you must dress for dinner; I promise not to keep you long."

She moved to the chair across from him and sat down tentatively. As he reseated himself, she said, "My lord, before you say whatever it is you wish to say, I should like to apologize for my behavior this morning. Indeed, I tried to find you earlier to tell you how sorry I am—"

She stopped speaking suddenly as he raised one of his hands with the palm toward her, as if he would ward off her words. There was a crooked smile on his thin face. When she was silent, he said, "Excuse me for stopping you, Miss Demming, but the truth is, I asked you here so that *I* could apologize to *you*. I am afraid that having been away from society for many months, I have lost the

76

skill of making polite conversation. I beg you to forgive me."

"There is nothing to forgive, my lord. I spoke inadvisedly on a subject that is none of my concern."

"But I asked for your opinion, Miss Demming, and having done so, had no right to take umbrage at your answer. You are Tony's fiancée and will in the course of time be my sister-in-law. I don't wish to begin our relationship with a misunderstanding. Could we start again, do you think?"

Celia smiled a smile he could not see, one that said she appreciated his apology, pitied him for the hardships he had endured, and wanted more than anything to be on good terms with the brother Anthony loved. When she answered, the warmth of her smile was reflected in her voice. "I should like that above all things, Lord Wexford."

"Good. This morning, you offered to read to me."

"Yes, certainly. Should you like me to?"

"I would. And perhaps write a few things. But only when you can spare the time. You and Tony will be entertaining friends and will have many demands placed upon you. Even now, I fear you should be dressing for dinner."

"Yes. I must go. But I can come for an hour or more in the morning, when Anthony goes riding."

"I shall expect you then. Good night, Miss Demming."

"Good night, my lord."

The following morning at breakfast Anthony raised the subject of Celia's reading to his brother.

"It was generous of you to offer. I know he feels cut off from everything and everyone."

"I can't imagine how he gets through even one day," Celia agreed. "He can't do any of the things he is accustomed to doing, not ride, nor drive, nor even walk about without someone to accompany him."

"He had taken over the management of the estate since my father's illness," Tony added. "That will be difficult for him now. I offered to help, but he assured me that he will deal with it."

"Is Lord Walsh's agent trustworthy?"

"He is, but an agent cannot be indefinitely on his own. Which reminds me—I have spoken to the head groom and have set up a carriage for your use: a phaeton and a pair of bays." As Celia's face broke into a pleased smile, he added provocatively, "You may take me for a drive, and I shall decide whether or not you may be trusted with them."

Answering in the same teasing tone, she said, "Only two horses? I would ever so much more impress the neighbors with a team of four."

"When I am convinced that your mother was not exaggerating your abilities, I'll let you try your hand at my curricle team."

Impulsively she leaned forward and grasped his hand where it lay on the table. "Thank you so much, Tony. It will be wonderful having a carriage. I will take your mother to the village. She said she so enjoys an open-air drive. And perhaps even Lord Wexford might like to get out—"

Anthony laughed, at the same time leaning forward to take her chin in his hand. "Easy there, my girl. Not so fast. First you will drive me, then perhaps Mother. Don't count on Robert, though. To my knowledge he has never in his life been driven by a female."

His hand slid down to the side of her neck, while his thumb traced the line of her jaw. The laughter died from his voice, and his words were soft, "You're sweet, you know, truly sweet, and ever so easy to please." He leaned forward to kiss her, his lips warm and tantalizing.

At first embarrassed by her lack of skill in kissing, Celia had slowly gained confidence. Now she responded readily, for each kiss had been more exciting than the last. She suspected that her tutelage by Tony held great promise for the future.

When Anthony left to go riding, Celia made her way to the book room. Lord Wexford was seated near the fire in company with Lady Aylesbury. Both rose as Celia entered.

"And here is Miss Demming, Robert, precisely on schedule. I will leave you to your tasks."

"You need not go, my lady," Celia protested. "I can come another time."

"No, no, my dear. As you can see, Robert has a rather formidable stack of correspondence on the desk. I will not keep him from his responsibilities. Adieu." With no more than that, she departed.

"I did not mean to drive her away," Celia said quietly.

"Nor did you," Wexford responded. "She does exactly as she pleases and always has."

When he said nothing more, she moved toward the desk. "Did you indeed wish me to aid you with the post?"

"Yes, but before we start on that, there is something else that I should like you to do for me."

He paused, and she said nothing, only stood regarding him, waiting for him to continue.

"Tony has the casualty lists from Waterloo. The ones he perused so diligently looking for some hint of my fate. They are on the table near the windows." Celia glanced in the direction of the table and saw there the pile of papers he described. "I should like you to read me the officers' casualty lists."

Celia inhaled quickly at this request, her face puckering in a troubled frown as she protested, "Are you quite certain, my lord? You have only just come home, and you're not strong. Surely it can wait a few days."

In a patient voice, almost as if he had expected this objection from her, he said, "I need to know which of my friends are dead, and which have survived. Not knowing plagues me continuously, and I cannot put my mind to other matters. If it is too onerous a task for you, I could ask Tony—"

"No. You need not ask him. I will read the lists to you. It's only that I—" She broke off, unable to say what she was thinking—that she did not wish to cause him more pain when he had been through so much already.

"Please, Lord Wexford, won't you sit."

He reseated himself in the chair near the fire while she retrieved the lists from the table and came to sit near him. A glance at his face told her he was settled to listen, so she started at the beginning of a list of officers. She read slowly, often glancing up to gauge Lord Wexford's response to what he was hearing. He said nothing, but strong emotion contorted his face: his jaw alternately contracted and relaxed, his brows wrinkled in sadness or disbelief, his unseeing eyes glistened. She knew he was remembering the faces, young or old, that went with the names she read.

"Captain Sir William Hyatt—"

"Not William." Celia broke off abruptly as this quiet near moan issued from his lordship. She looked up to see that he had bowed his head, covering his eyes with one hand.

She leaned forward compassionately and placed her hand tentatively on his knee. "My lord, please, surely we have done enough for today?"

He lifted his head and patted her hand, then picked it up, gently pressed it, and held it in his own. "You're right. It's enough for now. We can do more tomorrow."

"Sir William?" she asked.

"He was a close friend of Tony's, twenty-five, perhaps twenty-six years of age. I spoke to him the morning of the battle. He was so keen for a fight. So eager to grasp glory."

"And he did, my lord. As did all the men who served . . . or died."

There was a pause before he replied, "Yes. Yes, of course they did."

Celia spent the next twenty minutes opening and reading aloud the viscount's correspondence, making appropriate notes on a separate sheet when he asked her to. It seemed to Celia that the large majority of the items were tradesmen's bills.

This orderly disposal of the post was interrupted when the door burst open suddenly and a tall, dark-haired, and extremely handsome man stood upon the threshold. "My God," he ejaculated. "It is true. Robert! It's a bloody miracle!"

The viscount had come to his feet the moment he heard the man's voice. Now he smiled broadly as the newcomer crossed the room in several giant strides and grasped Wexford first by the hand, then by the shoulders, as if by touching him he would be convinced that it was no ghost he saw.

"John!" Wexford replied. "You old reprobate. Mind your tongue. Can't you see there is a lady present?"

Celia had the pleasure of seeing the handsome stranger's discomfiture as he turned to face her. "Indeed, ma'am, I sincerely apologize. I did not see you there. I had eyes only for my cousin."

At this Wexford laughed aloud. "You sink deeper and deeper into shame, John. To tell a lovely lady that you did not notice her. What will you say next? Miss Demming, before he offends beyond forgiveness, allow me to present my cousin, John Hardy. John, this is Tony's fiancée, Miss Celia Demming."

Mr. Hardy took the hand Celia offered and gallantly raised it to his lips. "Your servant, ma'am. For the sake of our soon-to-be relationship, I beg you to forgive my earlier rudeness. I meant no offense."

She smiled. "None was taken, sir. I am happy to make your acquaintance."

Mr. Hardy turned his attention back to the viscount, seeming unable to believe the evidence of his own eyes. "Oh, Rob," he said, "it's so good to have you back."

At exactly ten minutes before two, Celia descended the wide stairway to the great hall. She wore a midnight blue riding habit of soft wool that accentuated the delicacy of her complexion. When she had traveled halfway down the final flight, Anthony appeared from the salon below. Seeing her, he crossed the hall to wait at the bottom of the stairs.

Celia stopped, a soft flush tingeing her face at the memory of her previous ill-fated descent to a waiting Anthony.

He held out a hand to her and smiled his most charming smile. "That night, I remember thinking no one could look lovelier," he said. "I was wrong. You are lovelier now."

Her flush deepened but she smiled, descending the final stairs to put her hand into his. "I can't believe you ever wanted to see me again after the way I disgraced myself."

"It was an accident; it could have happened to anyone." He threaded her arm through his and walked with her across the hall to the front door. "You are riding to the orphanage with Ursula?"

"Yes. She promised I would be home in good time for dinner."

As if on cue, Ursula appeared at that moment, trotting up the drive on her brown gelding. While the groom holding Celia's horse helped her to mount, Anthony took hold of Ursula's bridle. "Shale will ride with you," he said, indicating the groom beyond his shoulder.

Ursula bristled visibly. "Come, Tony. We don't need a groom to ride two miles."

"It would please me, Ursula, if you would take him along."

Looking far from pleased at the prospect, Ursula nevertheless capitulated. "Very well, we will take him." Then, lowering her voice so that only Anthony could hear, she said, "I know how precious Miss Demming is to you, Anthony. Do you think I would let any harm come to her?"

"No, I know you wouldn't." He released her bridle and stepped back as the groom mounted. Celia turned to smile at Tony, and he raised his hand in farewell as the three set off down the drive.

Celia and Ursula rode side by side along the same track Celia and Anthony had taken the day he proposed to her. Layers of fallen yellow elm leaves lay thick on the road before them.

Ursula spoke of the orphanage in response to Celia's questions. "Lord Walsh bought the property when it came on the market many years ago and donated it for the orphanage. It's a small manor house tucked into a wooded valley. There is an excellent garden plot nearby, and Lord Walsh never minded if the children explored his woodland or fished in the streams."

"Will Lord Wexford be as generous when the land belongs to him?"

Ursula gave Celia a long considering look. "I have no reason to believe he won't be. I know that

Lady Walsh believes her husband will recover, but the truth is that the doctor says he is very weak and may not last the month."

As they rounded a sharp turn in the road, the small red brick manor came into view. It was a well-kept building in a charming autumnal setting, but the peace was disturbed by a bout of fisticuffs taking place on the tidy lawn before the house.

Celia barely had time to recognize what she was witnessing before both Ursula and the groom, Shale, had ridden forward, hurriedly dismounted, and thrown themselves into the altercation. Shale grasped one young ruffian by the shoulders while Ursula took the other around the waist and dragged him backward. Into the space they created stepped a woman of small stature, dressed entirely in sober black.

Celia, at first concerned for Ursula's safety, was surprised when both boys gave over fighting as soon as hands were laid upon them. Now they cast their eyes to the ground as the lady in black stared frigidly first at one, then the other.

Finally she spoke. "I am shocked—shocked. That two of my oldest children, those trusted to set an example, should behave in such a disgraceful fashion. And in front of a guest, as well."

At this mention of a visitor, both boys looked up guiltily, noticing Celia for the first time. Both immediately cast their eyes down again, shame turning their faces a bright red.

The lady in black spoke again. "Come with me, Thomas, and you, too, Harry. We will go inside and sit, and you two will settle this matter like gentlemen." Casting a fleeting smile at Celia and clearly expecting to be obeyed, she turned and walked into the house. The boys followed without a word.

"That is Mrs. Beebe," Ursula said. "I will introduce you when she is free. She is the matron here. She rules with a firm hand, but she is God-fearing and just, and more loving with children than anyone I have ever known. We are truly blessed to have her."

That day Celia enjoyed a guided tour of the orphanage and grounds given by Harry and Thomas, a task assigned them by Mrs. Beebe to make them forget their earlier disagreement and work together in harmony. Later Celia spent a pleasurable half hour reading to two six-year-old girls. She also carefully brushed and braided Kitty's hair, for although Kitty was twelve, she had a crippled hand and could not do the task herself. Celia's final chore for the afternoon was rocking a colicky infant boy until he went off to sleep.

On the ride home Celia was silent, and Ursula didn't press her. When they arrived at the Priory, Mr. Hardy was just returning as well. Celia greeted Tony's cousin, said good-bye to Ursula, and hurried inside to change for dinner. Ursula paused a few minutes in the drive to greet an old acquaintance.

"I assume you have come for the shooting, Mr. Hardy," she said. "You should have good sport this year. The birds are as thick as nobs in Mayfair."

He smiled. "Your scorn for Londoners is one of the few constants in my life, Miss Browne. It's good to see you, too. You have spent the afternoon with Miss Demming?"

"She went with me to the orphanage."

"Ah, did she indeed? And do you find her to be a silly, privileged, society belle?"

"Not at all. I find her to be deeply compassionate, genuinely kind and good."

"But not, of course, quite good enough for Tony."

At this rejoinder, Ursula flushed deeply and drew breath to respond, but all she replied was, "I must go. Good day, Mr. Hardy."

Without another word she wheeled her horse about and cantered off down the lane. John Hardy watched her retreating figure until she disappeared from sight. Only then did he turn and go into the house.

Chapter 7

THE NEXT MORNING Celia read for Lord Wexford again, continuing on the casualty lists she had started the day before. When they finished, she wondered whether Anthony had told him of the local men who had taken part in the battle. He was so determined to know who had perished, surely he should be told about his own people.

"I was with Ursula Browne yesterday, and she told me of the losses the village suffered at Waterloo. Has Anthony spoken to you?"

"No. Who? Not Ned Forbes."

"Yes. I'm afraid so. He lost a leg, poor man. But Miss Browne says he is recovering well and the family is getting by."

"Anyone else?"

"A man called Drew was killed."

"Damn!" This exclamation was half mumbled and quiet. "I should have known he would go. Why didn't I make him promise—swear to me that he would stay with his family?"

His reaction to the news of Mr. Drew's death was so intense that she found herself asking, "You knew him well?"

"We served together in the army when we were younger. He wanted to go when I volunteered this time, but I insisted that he stay with his wife and son. What will they do without him?"

His question was not directed at her; he seemed rather to be asking it of himself. Since Celia had an answer to hand, however, she offered it. "Miss Browne hoped to speak with you about them. She thought that Mrs. Drew could move into the village, and her son could find work in the quarry."

"Unacceptable," Wexford replied baldly. "I don't wish that boy apprenticed as a stonecutter. He is a farmer—loves farming. What can Ursula be thinking?"

Not knowing how to answer this question, Celia remained silent. When Wexford spoke, he changed the subject. "Have any more guests arrived?"

"The Crowthers and the Matlocks arrived last evening. The ladies seem most pleasant, and the gentlemen, eager to shoot."

"Jack Matlock is an old friend. It will be good to see him again."

"Why don't you come down for dinner?" Celia urged; then, seeing the immediate frown on Wexford's face, amended her suggestion. "After dinner, then."

"Perhaps, some evening. Not tonight. I am, in fact, a bit fatigued, Miss Demming."

Celia rose immediately. "Of course, my lord. I have stayed too long. Shall I come again tomorrow?"

"You have not stayed too long, and yes, please come again. You are the bright spot in my day."

As Celia walked down the hall to her own room, she reasoned that if she was the bright spot, the remainder of his day must be dreary indeed.

In her room she sat at the elegant French writing desk and scribbled two letters. The first was to her mother, relating the events of the past few days. She knew her mother would not be pleased to hear of Viscount Wexford's return, since Anthony could not inherit the earldom so long as his brother was alive. Celia, however, was content with the situation exactly as it was. She had Anthony; Anthony had his brother safely restored; Wexford had resumed his rightful place. All seemed right and proper to her.

Celia's second letter was directed to her father in Yorkshire. She apprised him also of Lord Wexford's return and her activities in Buckinghamshire. Then she made two requests of him with no question in her mind that he would comply with them at his earliest convenience. She placed the letters with her reticule. She would post them when she drove with Tony later in the day.

When Celia walked with Anthony to the stables that afternoon, she saw a sturdy phaeton (not the high-perch vehicle she would have liked) drawn up in the brick-paved yard. She could find no fault, however, with the magnificent bays harnessed between the shafts.

"Shall I take them while they are fresh?" Anthony asked, ready to hand her to the passenger seat.

"Absolutely not," she replied. "How can I prove my ability once they have settled to their work?"

"Very well," he answered. "You may take them from the start. I'm placing life and limb in your hands, miss. I hope you have a care with me."

She smiled at him as she took the reins and whip. "It is my plan always to take the greatest care of you—as you must know." She nodded to the groom who was holding the pair, and they moved out of the stable yard at a brisk trot.

Within a few minutes, any fears Anthony may have had concerning Celia's skill as a whip were dispersed. She handled the team expertly: feathered a turn to perfection, slowed to a safe speed when passing close to pedestrians, and easily controlled the younger horse's inclination to shy at a sudden flurry of windblown leaves.

They drove to High Wycombe, a town of sufficient size to enable Celia to buy both the sweets Lady Walsh desired and the supply of yarn that Celia herself sought. On impulse she purchased a scrap of pink ribbon that she would tie into Kitty's hair the next time she brushed it for her.

The passage through town of the smart carriage drew no little attention from passersby. Anthony was well-known here, in the closest town of any size to his home. Some people stopped to stare, others turned to speak to their companions. They had heard of Mr. Graydon's engagement; this, no doubt, was his intended bride. Beautiful, indeed, and driving herself behind a well-bred pair.

On the return trip, Celia graciously ceded the

reins to her companion, giving herself leisure to survey the colorful countryside.

"May I be trusted to drive your mother, sir?" she asked quite formally.

. He laughed. "Yes, you may." Then, more seriously he added, "But always take a groom, promise me."

"I promise. If you are not with me, I shall always have a strong-armed substitute in your place."

The following day was Sunday. When the morning dawned bright and clear, Celia asked Lady Walsh if she would care to drive with her to morning services in Little Graydon.

On their way back to the Priory, Celia took a roundabout route to prolong their drive. Their road followed the crest of a ridge, offering an excellent view of the broad deep valley below.

"This is lovely, my dear," Lady Walsh exclaimed, "so lovely. Soon the frost and cold will come and such excursions will be impossible. Thank you so much for suggesting it."

Celia made an appropriate response, then slowed her horses to a walk as her attention was captured by a movement in the valley below. Barely visible through the thinning leaves was a picturesque farmstead: solid stone cottage surrounded by neatly tilled fields. Near the cottage stood a carriage with a driver in the seat. Beside the cottage door stood a man and a woman engaged in conversation.

"Is that not Lord Wexford, my lady, before that cottage?"

Looking in the direction Celia indicated, Lady

Walsh said merely, "My dear, my eyes are not what they once were. I cannot say."

"But I didn't know he was getting out of the house. Do you think him strong enough?"

"If he is out, then he must feel he is able, child. That is the Drew cottage. No doubt he heard about her husband and felt he must call. It is his duty, after all, in his father's place, of course."

Lady Walsh said nothing more, and Celia let the subject drop. She sincerely hoped Lord Wexford had not done himself any injury by venturing out too soon. Perhaps she should not have told him about Mr. Drew. Perhaps she knew now why Anthony had said nothing.

That same evening the last guest, Trevor Farr, arrived. He had driven down from London and spent some time after dinner sharing the latest news from Town. Lord Wexford still had put in no appearance downstairs, but each of the houseguests had visited with him briefly.

During the days that followed, the household fell into a general pattern of activity. The men, and any of the ladies who wished to join them, rose early to go riding. During that time, Celia would meet with Lord Wexford. Later in the day, when the men went off to shoot, the ladies would gather in the salon or the morning room to chat or do needlework. If the weather was clement, some preferred a walk through the grounds. Celia occasionally took up passengers or ran errands to Little Graydon or High Wycombe.

The entire company would then gather for dinner. Afterward there would be cards or conversation, musical entertainments, and often the charades Lady Walsh had spoken of. These were entered into enthusiastically by all present. Celia soon discovered she was no more than a passable player, but no one seemed to mind. They agreed, one and all, that she would improve with practice.

Each night she retired to her rooms with a smile on her face. She could never remember spending time in such congenial company.

Lady Walsh joined the ladies each afternoon and was present for dinner each night. She invariably retired soon afterward to sit with her husband. There had been no change in his condition.

Celia continued to meet with Wexford each morning except Sundays. They had been sorting through heaps of correspondence that had piled up during his absence, deciding which could be thrown away, which must be attended to. When she came to a dressmaker's bill, unpaid since June, he rose impatiently.

"Good God. My mother has a handsome independence of her own. Is she so occupied she must leave a bill unpaid for five months? Give it to Carter to pay with the others. How much more of this must we do?"

She glanced up at his exasperated face. "Not much, only a few more. Once we have caught up, it will be a simple matter day to day."

"You shouldn't be doing it at all. It's not your responsibility. You're young, and there's a house full of company. You should be with them."

"I don't mind helping; I enjoy being useful. It's the least I can do for—"

When she broke off, he finished the sentence for her. "The least you can do for a helpless blind man."

She stood and fired back at him, "No. That wasn't what I was about to say. I intended to say it is the least I can do for you."

"Then why didn't you say it?"

"Because it sounded too much like pity."

"And you don't pity me?"

"No."

"Please, be honest, Miss Demming. You have been to this point."

"All right. Yes. I do pity you, but not in the way you think, and not for the reasons you think. You all gave so much for us, risked so much for us when you went away to fight. This is something I can do for you. Too little, not nearly enough, never enough. But I am grateful for the opportunity to show you, if not Mr. Drew and Ned Forbes, what your sacrifice meant to me, meant to all of us."

When she stopped, he did not respond, and after a few moments she said, "I try to imagine what it must have been like—"

"Don't, for you will never succeed. The imagination cannot conjure up such horror."

"And you think about it all the time."

"Waking and sleeping."

"You were in battles in Spain. They faded with time."

"Yes. But without sight, without the opportunity to see your lovely face, or a sunset, or the rise of a bird from the undergrowth, I find that all I see are those same scenes over and over again. The face of my friend George Wainwright as he died in my arms, the broken and bleeding bodies of the men in my command, the thick smoke, the noise, the carnage caused by volley after volley of heavy artillery. . . ."

His voice trailed off, and for a long moment neither spoke. Finally Celia could bear the silence no longer. "How can I help?" she asked.

"Take me for a drive."

"Tony says you have never been driven by a woman."

"True enough. But as long as I can't see, it shouldn't be too terrifying for me."

She smiled despite the gravity of their earlier conversation. "You are cruel, sir."

He seemed to consider. "Perhaps. I will decide that when the drive is over."

"Let's go now, before you change your mind," she said. "I'll order the carriage and be back for you in ten minutes. You'll need a coat. There's a chill in the air."

She was gone before he could reply. He rang for Gregson to fetch his greatcoat and was waiting at the top of the stairway when Celia came from her room. He offered his arm, which she took, and with his opposite hand on the banister, they descended the stairs together.

The carriage with the bay horses was already waiting outside. When Celia stopped beside the phaeton, Wexford said, "Allow me to hand you up, Miss Demming."

"Thank you, my lord," she said as she took his arm for balance and climbed into the carriage.

As he walked unassisted around the back to the other side, he asked, "What vehicle is this?"

"It is your old phaeton, my lord," the groom answered. "Mr. Anthony thought it would do for the young lady."

"I'm surprised the mice haven't eaten it through."

"Not at all," Celia said. "It polished up beautifully and is most respectable."

As Wexford pulled himself up and settled beside her, she said, "Where shall I drive you, my lord?"

"I shall direct you, Miss Demming, to one of the most charming drives in the neighborhood. That is, if Tony hasn't already taken you there. We shan't need you, Shale."

The groom released the horses and stepped aside as they moved past him. Celia could see from his expression that he would have preferred to accompany them, but she could say nothing to contradict Lord Wexford's orders.

"Turn left outside the gates. In a mile when the road divides, take the left fork. Has Tony taken you that way?"

"No. I don't believe so."

They drove for more than an hour. He directed, and as she described the landmarks, he pointed out each farm, each hillside, each tree that held a memory of Tony. "We went sledding there one year after a heavy snowfall. . . . Do you see the tall elm that overhangs the water meadow? Tony fell from that one when he was about ten. I told him not to climb it."

During the entire drive, they never once spoke of the army or of Waterloo. When they had arrived home and were ascending the stairs together, she asked, "Will you drive with me again?"

"Certainly. I was not frightened in the least."

She turned to see him smiling, then added impulsively, "Come down after dinner tonight. All of your friends miss you. Each night someone mentions that the gathering is not the same without you." They had reached the top of the stairs. She turned and placed both hands on his arm. "Please say yes. I'll come up and fetch you myself after dinner."

Her voice was so eager, her grip so insistent that he yielded to her entreaty. "All right. I will come down, but I won't bide till the wee hours as you all do."

"Certainly not. No one would expect it. Till after dinner, then."

Celia left him at the door to his room. He looked tired. She hoped he would rest.

Celia had missed luncheon, but she wasn't hungry. She collected the yarn she had purchased on her drive with Anthony and hurried downstairs to join the other ladies in the India sitting room. It was given this name for good reason. The carved furnishings and brightly colored wall hangings, even the carpets and ivory knickknacks were Indian, collected and displayed by a younger Lady Walsh during her period of enchantment with India and all things Indian. Celia suspected that some of the carpets, in particular, were very valuable. They certainly were beautiful.

The other ladies were all there before her: Lady

Walsh, the Viscountess Aylesbury, Lady Matlock, and Emily Crowther. Ursula, who often joined the party in the evening, seldom visited in the afternoon.

"You are late, my dear," Lady Aylesbury remarked. "Could it be that you were driving with my nephew?"

Celia smiled resignedly. It seemed to her that nothing in the household escaped the viscountess's notice. "I was indeed. How did you know?"

"I saw you leaving myself, from the window in the salon."

Noticing the very beginning of a knitting project in Celia's lap, Emily Crowther asked, "What is that you are starting, Miss Demming, a muffler?"

"No, indeed. I am starting a sock." Four pairs of eyes were lifted toward her.

Lady Matlock said, "How curious. I have never made a sock."

"Nor I," Emily added. "I wouldn't know how."

"I didn't either," Celia replied, "but I asked Mrs. Beebe, and she gave me a few quick instructions. Then I borrowed this sample from one of Lord Walsh's grooms." She held up a coarse gray sock, well-worn but clean. "I don't think it will be too difficult."

"Who is Mrs. Beebe?" Lady Matlock asked.

"The matron at the Little Graydon orphanage," Lady Walsh answered. "I assume you plan the socks for the children, Celia," she continued. "Is the need great?"

"It is, my lady. Most of the ones they have are

worn into holes; some of the older children have none at all."

Lady Walsh nodded her head knowingly. "If you give me some yarn and teach me the pattern, I will help you."

Emily Crowther looked down at the delicate silk embroidery in her lap. "I promised this pillow covering to my aunt, but as soon as it is finished, you must teach me as well."

Celia possessed an evening gown fashioned of deep turquoise satin. Her mother had ordered it to be made up during the campaign for Lord Trevanian. Since he was rumored to fancy green, Mrs. Demming hoped he might admire Celia in this particular shade. Celia had never worn the gown. When it was finished and she tried it on, her mother declared it to be "too fast" and hung it away in the wardrobe.

Celia wondered now why her mother had sent it along. Perhaps now that Celia was safely engaged, the frugal Mrs. Demming thought the dress could see some use.

Celia took it from the wardrobe and fingered the sleek satin. If she was honest, she had to admit that she had never cared for the pale pinks, soft yellows, and several tones of white that her mother felt suitable to her position. She had been thrilled when her mother chose this particular fabric and downcast when she was not permitted to wear it.

Since that first horrible evening when she could not decide what to wear, she had simply instructed Wylie to lay out something appropriate. Now she carefully spread the turquoise dress across the foot of her bed. Tonight she would choose for herself. She would wear the turquoise gown.

When Wylie entered the room some minutes later and saw the gown, she said, "You will wear this tonight, Miss Celia?"

"Yes. If you think it suitable."

"It is most beautiful, miss."

Celia had to agree. Once the dress was on and her hair carefully arranged, she felt sophisticated indeed. In the corridor outside her room, she met Mr. Hardy on his way downstairs.

He stopped and bowed, a smile lighting his handsome face. "How lovely you look this evening, Miss Demming. May I escort you down?"

"I would be delighted, sir," she replied as she linked her arm in his.

Most of the houseguests were already gathered in the drawing room when Celia and John Hardy made their entrance. When they came in, all heads turned in their direction and conversation ceased. For one lowering moment, Celia thought she had made a dreadful mistake in wearing the turquoise dress. It did not occur to her to consider what a stunning couple she and her handsome, impeccably dressed companion made.

When Anthony came toward them, her concerns fled. There was no disapproval in his face, only admiration. "How beautiful you look tonight, Celia. What a striking gown!" Then, with a glance at his cousin, he added, "And you, John, are no less splendid; you cast us all in the shade."

Mr. Hardy surrendered Celia to Tony, then

twitched the lace at one wrist straight. "One must not allow one's standards to slip, dearest Anthony, even in the country."

Then as John was about to walk away, Celia detained him. "Please wait, Mr. Hardy. There is something I wanted both you and Anthony to be aware of. Today, when I was with Lord Wexford, he said that he might come down to join the company after dinner tonight. If he does, I think it is important for your guests to know that they should not mention the recent hostilities. He told me that it is all he thinks about, all he sees in his mind's eye. He even dreams of the battle. He needs relief from that; he needs to think of other things, speak of other things."

"I will be certain that everyone is aware," John replied. "And thank you, Miss Demming, you have accomplished what Tony and I could not."

"I'm not sure he will come," she said, "but I'm hoping he will. I told him I would come myself to fetch him after dinner."

Chapter 8

WHEN THE DINNER had concluded, the ladies adjourned to the drawing room, leaving the gentlemen to their port. Shortly thereafter, Celia excused herself and went upstairs to see if Lord Wexford was still willing to come down. When she arrived outside his door, it stood half open. From inside she could hear Wexford's voice raised impatiently, "Go away, Gregson, this task is beyond your power."

Celia stepped into the open doorway and knocked lightly on the door. She saw instantly what the problem was. Gregson was attempting to tie the viscount's neckcloth. From the pile of discarded attempts on the floor beside them, it was clear he had met with difficulty.

"Is there anything I can do to help?" she asked as the valet turned toward the door.

"Good evening, Miss Demming," Wexford said as he pulled the latest ruined neckcloth and cast it aside like the others.

"I'm so pleased you've decided to come down," she said pleasantly, as she walked into the room. "Here. Allow me to help you with that." Gregson folded another neckcloth and positioned it about the viscount's neck.

"I can do it from this point, Gregson," she said. "I occasionally help my father with this task. I can do only one simple style, but I flatter myself that the result is respectable."

As Celia stepped forward to take the cloth into her own hands, Wexford said, "You may go, Gregson."

"And your coat, my lord?"

"Miss Demming will help me."

"Very good, sir."

Gregson then disappeared into the adjoining dressing room.

Celia concentrated on her work, her fingers pressing delicate creases into the starched muslin. "Now, if you will stand quite still, my lord, I believe I can accomplish something that will satisfy you. You will note I say satisfy, not please, for my skills, as I said, have their limits. I must warn you, however, that your cousin, Mr. Hardy, will outshine you tonight. He has a splendid waterfall this evening."

He burst out laughing. "I have always stood in John's magnificent shadow, ma'am. That will be nothing new." Then more seriously he added, "You are quite amazing, you know."

Her fingers paused as she looked from her task up into his face. "And how is that, my lord?"

"I was ready to forget the whole evening when you arrived. Now here you have me wondering how I shall measure up to John."

"I don't think a single one of your friends will

even notice your cravat, my lord. You have come home safely, and that's all they care about."

He grew silent while she continued with her task. When she stood so close, he could tell more precisely how tall she was from the direction of her voice. There was a rustling of her gown as it brushed his legs, and a hint of lavender rose from her hair.

"What color is your hair?" he asked.

Her fingers hesitated again, as she looked up in surprise. "Auburn, dark auburn."

"And your eyes?"

"Green, slightly gray in some light."

He nodded and said nothing more.

When Celia had finished, she said, "There, I have done. Now, feel for yourself and see if I have done a fair job."

He raised his hand carefully and fingered the neckcloth. "A fair job indeed. Better than fair—an excellent effort."

"And you will not be ashamed to be seen by your friends?"

"Not at all."

"Good. Then we should go down. Where is your coat? Ah, here it is."

She collected his dark blue coat from the back of a chair and stood behind him as he slipped it on. Then she came around to the front to set it properly on his shoulders. She could see that it was still too big, for although the pallor of his face was diminishing a little each day, he did not appear to have gained any weight.

Satisfied with the set of the coat, she said, "If I could have your arm, my lord."

He offered it, and they went downstairs together. The gentlemen had joined the ladies by that time, and Celia noticed that they were all careful not to overwhelm the viscount when he entered. They came up to speak with him one or two at a time. She heard no one mention Waterloo.

Ursula had not joined the company for dinner, but Celia noticed that she was now present. In the first minutes after Celia returned with Wexford, she noticed Ursula sitting alone in the window seat. She smiled a greeting across the room to her and thought she saw tears in Ursula's eyes. No doubt she had strong feelings for Wexford, as indeed she had for Anthony and the entire family.

John Hardy, standing alone near the fireplace, noticed Ursula's distress. He crossed the room and sat beside her, offering his handkerchief.

"He's so thin," she said, dabbing her eyes.

"He will gain the weight back, in time. It would perhaps be best to control your tears, Miss Browne, especially in company."

She looked at him sharply, "Why? Robert cannot see them. Surely they don't offend you?" She stood suddenly, tossed his handkerchief into his lap, and walked away to stand where he had been earlier, gazing down into the fire.

The following day, when Celia joined Lord Wexford for their morning session, he had a gift for her.

"When I handed you down from the carriage the other day," he said, "I noticed that you had no driving gloves. I had my mother pick these up for you when she went into High Wycombe yesterday. I hope they fit." He handed over a pair of soft kid driving gloves.

"Oh, my lord, they are very fine. Thank you. And they fit perfectly. Look." Instantly realizing her mistake, she added hastily, "I'm sorry. That was so thoughtless."

"Don't be silly. It wasn't thoughtless. And I can look. Here, let me feel them." As he reached for her hands, she placed them in his. He handled them gently in his own, feeling each finger. "You're absolutely right. They are an excellent fit. When will you take me driving again? This afternoon?"

He could hear the regret in her voice as she said, "I can't this afternoon; I go to the orphanage today with Miss Browne. But we could go tomorrow."

"Tomorrow will be excellent, if the weather holds. What time?"

After they had settled the details of their drive, Celia read from the London papers then wrote several letters. When they had finished, he said, "When you see Ursula today tell her that all has been arranged concerning Mrs. Drew. She will stay on at her cottage, and Dan Hemple will work the land. Young Alan will come to work on the home farm."

"I'll tell her."

Celia and Ursula rode to the orphanage with Shale trailing along behind. This was their third trip together. They were quickly becoming friends.

Celia relayed Lord Wexford's message regarding Mrs. Drew and her son.

"If she stays in the cottage, how will she pay the rent?" Ursula asked.

"I don't know. Perhaps he won't ask her for any. He and her husband were friends."

"Seems peculiar to me," Ursula answered. "But it's his cottage—his decision."

"I hope to spend some time with Kitty today," Celia said. "I bought a hair ribbon for her and never even saw her on Monday."

"That was thoughtful of you," Ursula said. "What color?"

"Pink."

"She'll like that. I do wish I could hit upon a situation for Kitty. She worries me."

"Why?"

"Most of the girls her age have learned a skill. Some will be able to go into service. Others will be taken on by the farms that need extra help. But Kitty, with her bad hand, cannot be a maid. Most physical labor is beyond her ability. I don't know what will become of her."

"How did she come to the orphanage?"

"She was left as a small babe at the church. We don't think she is an orphan. Most likely her parents were poor and couldn't afford to raise a child who couldn't do its fair share of the work."

"How dreadful."

"Yes. But I think she has been happy with us. In two years, though, she will be fourteen, and by then something must be found for her."

Celia brushed and braided Kitty's hair later that

afternoon and delighted the child with the pink ribbon. But the whole time Celia couldn't help thinking of what Ursula had said. What would become of Kitty when she was too old to stay on at the orphanage?

After dinner that evening, the entire company was gathered in the drawing room having just chosen teams for charades when Wexford appeared accompanied by his cousin. Celia crossed to greet them at the door and exclaimed at the elegance of his lordship's cravat.

"John tied it for me," Wexford said, "while the men dawdled over their port. He calls it the 'Hardy Fall.'"

"But you are not a Hardy, sir," Celia exclaimed.

"No. But my mother was, so we will assume it to be an acceptable style for me."

Celia cast a look of gratitude at John for offering his services to his cousin. "Will you join our team for charades, Lord Wexford?" she asked. "We need another quick wit, for the other side already has both your cousin and Lord Matlock."

Before he could object, she led him to a sofa and sat beside him. Tony had taken a slip of paper from the bowl that held subjects to be portrayed. As soon as he looked at it, he said, "I need another person to help me. A lady. Have you any objection to that?"

When Lord Matlock, captain of the other team, raised no objection, Tony grasped Ursula's hand and pulled her to her feet, showing her the slip of paper upon which the clue was written.

Celia leaned close to Wexford and quietly told

him all she saw happening. "Tony has taken Ursula up to help him. He is pointing to himself, and to Ursula."

"You're two people," Lady Matlock said. "A couple."

"He has taken Ursula into his arms and is looking deep into her eyes," Celia continued.

"You're lovers," shouted Todd Crowther.

At Tony's vehement nod of approval, Celia said, "Tony has nodded yes, they are lovers. Now he is patting Ursula on the head. He looks positively demented. He is pointing to himself again, beating himself upon the breast."

"Antony and Cleopatra," Wexford said, loud enough for all to hear.

"Yes!" Tony shouted. "Our point."

Celia turned to Wexford in disbelief. "How did you guess that?"

"It was clear."

"Not to me it wasn't."

The game continued for several hours, the lead in points shifting back and forth between the teams more than once. As the hour advanced, the players grew bolder and noisier; sometimes the whole room dissolved in uncontrollable laughter. When they decided to call a halt near midnight, Celia didn't think either side any longer knew the score or even cared which team was the victor.

The following morning, when Celia was supposed to arrive to read for Wexford, the butler entered to say he had a message from her.

"What is the message, Leech?" Wexford asked.

"Miss Demming asked if you would please excuse her this morning, my lord, as Mr. Anthony is taking her to call on some of the neighbors; but she said she will be ready to drive at the time you arranged, and she will meet you at the head of the stairs."

"Thank you, Leech. Order my chestnut team harnessed to the curricle and have them at the door at two o'clock."

"Very good, my lord."

When Leech was gone, Wexford put aside the paper he was going to have Miss Demming read to him, and as he did so, he discovered he was ridiculously disappointed that she wouldn't be there that morning. He had to admit that of all the women he had ever known, she was the least complicated and most natural. She seemed to know instinctively how to put him at his ease, even when he himself wasn't certain why he was uneasy. Tony was lucky to have found her.

At precisely two o'clock, Celia found Lord Wexford waiting at the top of the stairway. In the drive outside the house was a curricle and a team of four horses.

She smiled with delight. "These are your chestnuts. Tony has told me about them. You will let me drive them?"

"I can't imagine who else."

"Perhaps Shale," she said, since the groom stood holding the leaders.

"Shale won't be coming with us. Will you, Shale?"

"No, my lord."

"There you have it, Miss Demming. Take the

reins. The privilege is all yours. Tony told me you have driven a curricle-and-four."

"Indeed. My father has a splendid team."

"These will challenge your skill. Honeysuckle is the outside leader. She'll try to run the show, test you every step of the way. On the other hand, Spring Mist, your inside wheeler, is as steady as they come. Take them out and see how you do."

The moment Shale released the leaders, Honeysuckle broke into a trot, and the others followed her lead. With Wexford's warning in mind, Celia was prepared, and after a short battle of wills, the lead horse settled into the walk Celia demanded of her.

"Good," Wexford approved. "You have shown her you're not a novice. She will respect you now."

For the first fifteen minutes of the drive, Celia's attention was totally claimed by the fresh team, for although they were well-matched and well-mannered, they knew they had a strange driver.

Eventually they settled into a steady, ground-covering trot, and Celia marveled at their stamina.

"Should you like to let them gallop?" he asked.

"I would love to. But I'm not at all certain I could stop them once I let them run."

"What's the road like ahead?" he asked.

"Straight and wide and empty for as far as I can see."

"Go ahead then, let them run. I'll lend a hand if you need help pulling them in."

So Celia did let them run, and they ran straight and true down the center of the road, pulling the curricle like a feather behind them. When she saw a bend in the road far ahead, she said, "I will pull them in now, my lord. There is a turn in the distance."

Her first attempt to collect the team slowed them, but they did not fall into the trot she wanted. She experienced one short moment of panic, thinking she would not be able to stop them, before she felt Wexford feeling for her hands and the reins she held.

"It is not so much a question of strength as skill," he said. "Don't let go. Keep up the tension behind my hands and try to feel what I'm doing."

By now he had a firm grip on the reins above her hands, and in a matter of seconds, with steady, firm pressure, the team gave over their headlong rush and dropped again into a manageable trot.

"I have never in my life traveled so swiftly," she said.

"Did you like it?"

"Yes. It was wonderful. Like flying."

Then, as she realized he was still holding her hands, an indefinable shiver ran through her and she said, "I have them now, my lord. Thank you. I must say, I truly needed the help."

"I'm not so sure," he said as he freed her hands. "I think in a moment or two more you would have had them slowed all by yourself."

"Isn't it frightening for you," she asked, "rushing along at such speed, not being able to see where you are going?"

"No. It's not in the least frightening. It takes a lot to frighten you once you have taken part in a battle of any size at all."

"I'm sorry. I shouldn't—"

"Miss Demming," he said, interrupting her. "Please stop the horses."

When she had pulled them in and the carriage came to a standstill, he turned slightly toward her on the seat. "Miss Demming, there are two things I should like to settle with you. The first is that I would like you to stop apologizing to me every time you mention the army, or my loss of sight. These things are nothing you should apologize for. We were engaged in a bloody conflict. Every family, every village in the country was affected. It is on everyone's mind and on their tongues. It will be mentioned; you cannot stop it. And I, my dear, can deal with it. Trust me, I can."

"And the second thing?" she asked in a rather small voice.

"Please, *please* call me Robert. In a few short months I will be your brother-in-law. I find it incongruous that you are tying my neckcloth one moment and calling me Lord Wexford the next."

"I will strike a bargain with you, sir. I will call you Robert if you will call me Celia, but only in private with the family."

"Agreed, for now."

When she had started the team again, this time at a leisurely walk, he asked, "How was your visit to the orphanage yesterday?"

"Rewarding, and a bit troubling."

"Why troubling?"

"For one thing, the wood supply is low, and the nights are getting colder."

"I'll speak to Carter, he will see that they have

whatever they need to see them through the winter."

"That would be wonderful."

When she said nothing more, he asked, "What else? You said for one thing, which means there must be more that troubles you."

"There is a young girl, Kitty, who is twelve. She has a crippled, useless hand, and Ursula says she will be unable to find work like the other girls. I worry what will become of her."

"No doubt she'll end up at the posting inn at High Wycombe," he said. "Girls like her often do. She can serve customers with her good hand, and for the work that comes afterward, she won't need her hands at all."

For a moment Celia had no idea what he was talking about. Then, as his meaning dawned on her, she was so shocked she could barely speak. "You mean . . . surely you can't mean . . . she wouldn't be . . ."

"A prostitute, yes."

She stared at him in horror. "I wish, my lord . . . Robert . . . that you could see me right now."

"And why is that?"

"Because I would like you to see the shock on my face. How can you even suggest such a thing?"

"I suggest it because it is a reality. And I am, my dear Celia, a realist. I have been forced to be."

"But surely there can be some other answer for her."

"Should you like me to give her a house and an income, or perhaps a dowry?"

"Of course not, but there must be something—"

"You have seen the estate records," he said. "My father lived beyond his means for years. That kind of extravagance cannot be remedied overnight. I cannot afford to pension off every dependent who has a crippled hand or a missing leg. And, believe me, I know exactly what they are suffering. If the girl can't use her hand, and you don't want her to be forced to sell her body, then think of some way she can use her brain to make her way in the world."

"What do you mean?" Celia asked.

"You said she is twelve. That means she still has a few years in which to acquire some training, some sort of education. Is she intelligent? Can she learn?"

"I think she is very clever, yes," Celia replied.

"Then she must learn to read, learn her figures."

Already Celia's mind was racing ahead. "If I taught her to read, she could teach the others."

"If *you* taught her?"

"Yes. Who else? If she learned, and could teach the others, that would free Mr. Browne and Ursula both to do other things. Then Kitty would be useful, and perhaps Mrs. Beebe would allow her to stay on at the orphanage."

"Don't be so sure Ursula wants to be relieved of her duties."

"I know she has no wish to be, but surely she will soon marry and have children of her own. She will have less time then to give to charitable work."

"I think your idea is a good one," he approved. "But I believe you should discuss it with Ursula be-

116

fore you do anything. She may see a problem you have not considered."

"I will. I will speak with her first."

When they arrived at the stable yard, they met Tony and John Hardy on their way to the house. As a groom took the leaders, Tony reached up to hand Celia out of the carriage. "Shale told us you had taken the curricle," he said. "Did you have a good drive?"

"It was wonderful, Tony. They run like the wind. I had a delightful time."

"I must say, Miss Demming," John added, "that you are a most fortunate female. I would have wagered a monkey that Wexford would never let any woman handle his cattle."

"Ah, but Celia is not just any woman," Tony replied. "Is she, Robert?"

"Certainly not," Wexford said. "She is an excellent whip. It is an honor to be driven by her."

Chapter 9

THE NEXT DAY was Sunday. Celia rose early to dress for services. She had promised to drive Lady Walsh again if there was no rain. She finished dressing in good time, dismissed Wylie, then decided to wait for Lady Walsh downstairs. She collected her warm pelisse, picked up her driving gloves and reticule, and stepped quietly into the hall. The house was quiet; she suspected that most of the guests were still asleep.

She closed the door softly and had taken no more than two steps down the hall when a loud shattering sound echoed behind her. This was quickly followed by a muffled thump and a string of oaths. As there was no question that these sounds originated within Lord Wexford's bedchamber, Celia anxiously stepped to his door, which stood slightly open, and knocked. "Lord Wexford? Gregson?"

When she received no answer, she pushed the door wider to call again and immediately saw the cause of the noise. Dropping her things near the door, she hurried across the room. Wexford was sitting on the floor in a puddle of water amid the broken shards of a large pitcher and basin. He was in his bare feet, wearing breeches but no shirt.

"Robert! What happened?" she cried, uncertain whether she should hurry to help him or turn her face away from the half-naked man. When she saw that his wrist was bleeding, she made up her mind. She stepped carefully over the shards and bent to help him.

"I knocked over the damned ewer," he said. "Then I slipped in the water and fell. This leg is so stiff, I can't seem to get up."

"I'm not surprised," she said, all business. "It's your wounded leg you've fallen on. It must hurt dreadfully. Shall I get Tony?"

"No. Don't wake him. I feel a complete fool. If you will give me your arm, I think I can find my balance."

She offered her arm, and he leaned on her heavily, managing to get to his feet.

"I'm not hurting you?" he asked.

"No. But now that you're standing, you mustn't move. There is broken pottery all about your feet. Stand still until I pick it up."

"You can't do that. You'll cut yourself."

"Nonsense. They are big pieces." She bent and quickly cleared a path between him and the bed.

As she took his arm and led him there, she noted that his limp was pronounced. "I think you have hurt yourself, and I believe I must call Anthony."

"Please don't, but if you see my dressing gown about, I should like to have that."

This mention of his state of undress made her blush painfully. She was grateful he could not see her acute discomfort as she brought the gown to him and helped him into it. Never before in her life had she seen a man without his shirt. She felt ashamed to look, but could not tear her eyes away as he brought the ends of the gown together, tied the sash at his waist, then sat on the edge of the bed. Was Tony like that? All solid and muscular? She supposed he was. It made her shiver to think of it.

"Shall I ring for Gregson?" she asked. "You have a cut on your wrist."

"Where?"

"The right one. Let me see if it's serious."

He held out the arm, and she rolled back the long sleeve of the dressing gown to get a good look. "It's not too deep. I don't think it will need to be sutured, but it definitely must be dressed. Who shall it be, Tony or Gregson?"

"Tony. Gregson fusses like a mother hen."

"Stay where you are, then; I'll be back in a moment."

She hurried down the hall and knocked firmly on Anthony's door. He opened it a few seconds later. He was dressed in breeches and a fine white cambric shirt, open at the throat. His hair was still tousled from sleep, and one lock fell over his forehead. It made him look boyish and wonderfully appealing.

"Well, hello," he said when he saw who stood there.

"Good morning, Tony," she said, and smiled; then on impulse she rose on her tiptoes to kiss him on the mouth.

As the brief kiss ended, she said, "Robert has fallen and hurt his leg. He also has a cut that needs dressing."

He was through the door and closing it before she finished talking. They walked together through the silent corridors. She quietly explained what had happened, leaving out the part about Wexford's state of partial undress and ending with why she had come for him instead of ringing for Gregson.

When they got back to Robert's room, he was sitting where she had left him. As Tony examined the cut, she said, "I must go. I am driving Lady Walsh to church."

"Celia." It was Robert's voice, and his hand held out toward her, palm up. She placed her own in it, and he curled his fingers gently around hers. "Thanks for hearing, and thanks for coming to help. I would still be sitting there on the floor if not for you."

"I was happy to be of assistance. I only hope you haven't re-injured your old wound."

He released her hand, and she collected her things from the floor near the door. She cast a sympathetic look at Wexford, then glanced one final time at Tony. In his face she saw his unspoken thank-you, straight from the heart, so she smiled and then nodded and left.

When she arrived downstairs, Lady Walsh was not in evidence, nor had the coach been brought around to the drive. Celia decided to walk back to the stables to collect it herself. In the stable yard another carriage was ready and waiting. The driver appeared to be the man who had driven Lord Wexford to the Drew cottage the previous Sunday. Was that why Wexford had been up so early? Was he planning a drive again this morning? She wondered if he would still go after his mishap.

During the drive to church, Celia didn't mention Wexford's fall, for she saw no reason to worry the countess unnecessarily.

At the beginning of December, Lady Walsh planned to hold what she called an informal gathering to introduce Celia to the neighbors. There would be dinner followed by an evening of dancing, with the traditional supper at midnight.

When Celia saw the length of the guest list and the costly delicacies on the menu, she voiced her concern to Tony.

"Couldn't you convince her to shorten the guest list?"

"I doubt it. I'm sure she has invited everyone she feels she must, and would be appalled if I suggest eliminating even one person."

"Then the menu—surely she could offer less lavish fare?"

"You're worried about the cost?"

"Yes. It would trouble Robert, I know. And he doesn't need more worries on top of the problems he already has."

"I could offer to pay for this little gathering myself," Tony said, "but I think I know what he would say." When the frown on her face deepened, he added, "I'll talk to him. Maybe he'll let me pay half, at least."

In the end it turned out that Tony was right.

When applied to, Wexford insisted that Tony bore no responsibility for Lady Walsh's entertainments.

Having done all she could through Tony, Celia soon realized that she personally could do nothing further to curb Lady Walsh's extravagance. Being young and a lover of parties, she was soon drawn into the excitement herself.

Several days later when they returned from the orphanage, Celia invited Ursula up to her room to continue a discussion they had started during their ride.

Soon, however, Celia's thoughts turned to the party. "Help me to decide which gown I should wear," she said, going to the wardrobe and extracting two gowns, both equally lovely. "At first I thought the blue would be best, but Tony loves this mint green."

"I think the green is perfect, but I am not the one to advise you. I know nothing of fashion."

"You know what you like, and that's good enough for me," Celia responded. "What are you wearing?"

"I'm not coming."

Celia looked at her friend in surprise. "What do you mean you're not coming? You must come."

Ursula shook her head. "Big, fancy parties are not for me. I wouldn't be comfortable. I don't fit in."

"But that's nonsense. You are here nearly every night for dinner, and you fit in wonderfully."

"That's different. I know the houseguests well. They have come every year since I was seventeen."

"But you must come," Celia persisted. "There will be wonderful music, and dancing, and delectable food. I will enjoy myself ever so much more if you are here."

"You won't even miss me. You will be having such a good time yourself."

"And you would have a good time, too. I can't believe that you don't want to come."

"Even if I did want to, I have nothing appropriate to wear. My gowns are too outmoded for such a gathering."

"The blue gown you wore the other night would be perfect. I have a paisley shawl I could lend you that would look very handsome with it, and we could have Wylie do your hair in a new way."

Celia's hopes started to rise as Ursula seemed to consider her suggestions. "I suppose the blue would do . . . but . . . I have no slippers for dancing—"

"I will lend you some," Celia interrupted. "And gloves, too. And anything else you need. Please say you will come."

Swept along by Celia's enthusiasm, Ursula smiled resignedly and said, "All right. I'll think about it."

Later, when Wylie was applied to, she said she would be more than happy to dress Miss Browne's hair several ways to see if she could hit upon one that the young lady fancied. Wylie also suggested that the blue gown in question might be made to look smarter if the old lace trim was removed and new lace applied, perhaps in a slightly different shade or even a contrasting color. Ursula was so delighted by this suggestion that she spent several hours painstakingly removing the old lace in preparation for attaching the new.

Three days before the proposed party, Celia was

reading to Lord Wexford in the book room when a footman interrupted to say that some goods had arrived from Yorkshire for Miss Demming, and Leech needed to know her wishes concerning their disposition.

"Please tell Leech I will be down directly," she said, then waited until the footman had gone before she spoke again. "I had planned to discuss this with you, Robert, but I forgot."

"Tell me now."

"One of the first times I spoke with Ursula, she said that Mrs. Forbes wanted to take in some sewing. Then later, when I visited the orphanage, it occurred to me that if my father sent some bolts of wool, perhaps Mrs. Forbes could sew coats for the children and solve two problems at one time."

"I remember Tony saying that your father produces excellent wool."

"He does. I think it is the finest wool in Yorkshire. And along with the cloth, I had him send yarn, for I have been experimenting with making socks."

"For the children at the orphanage."

"Yes. And Emily Crowther and your mother have been helping me. Even Lady Matlock has put aside her embroidery and is trying her hand at knitting."

He smiled. "Now, *that* I would really love to see."

"I should have asked you before I wrote to my father, but I didn't know you well then, and I didn't feel comfortable speaking about it."

"There's no harm done. If the children need the clothing, then they should have it. Have your father send me an account—"

"Oh, no!" Celia interrupted. "He doesn't expect to be paid. I intend these goods to be a gift, from me and my family to the orphanage. Everyone else gives something; I would like to do my part."

"Very well. Then I thank you, as will Ursula and the Reverend Browne, and the children, too, when they are warm and comfortable this winter. You had best go. Leech will be pacing the hall wondering where you are."

"I'll be right back," she said. "I want to finish reading the article I started."

When she was gone, he turned his head and stared at the eastern-facing wall of the room. Celia had said the day was bright and sunny, and had asked permission to open the draperies for light to read by. As he gazed now at the wall, he had no difficulty distinguishing the slice of light entering at the window from the dark draperies flanking both sides. For nearly a week now, he had suspected that his light perception was improving. Now he was certain of it.

Celia soon returned and continued reading the paper. When she had finished, Wexford asked, "And how are preparations coming for the party? Is everything in readiness?"

"Everything seems ready but me. I find that the closer the day comes, the more nervous I grow."

"I can't see why. All those invited are friends and neighbors who wish you well."

"The Duchess of Multree will be here. I must admit, I am very anxious about meeting her. Tony says I should call her Aunt, but I can't see myself doing that. I would never have the courage."

"She is my father's sister, and Tony and I call her Aunt Louise, but I think perhaps it would be best for you to address her as Your Grace, at least until she invites you to use a more familiar form of address. She is not proud, but straitlaced—a stickler for proper decorum. It would be best not to fall down the stairs at her feet."

Celia blushed, thankful once again that he could not see her face. "I suppose Tony told you about that," she said in a small voice, the memory of that awful tumble still strong enough to embarrass her.

"He said he was totally captivated from that moment, and his feelings haven't wavered since."

Celia stood, suddenly uncomfortable listening to Robert speak of Tony's feelings for her.

When he heard her stand, he said, "Has our time passed already?"

"Not quite, but I must leave a bit early today. Emily Crowther and I plan to walk to the rectory with the socks we have finished. Mr. Browne visits the orphanage this afternoon and will take them along. I will come tomorrow at the regular time."

Nearly half an hour later, while Celia was changing from her dainty house slippers into serviceable walking shoes, there came a delicate scratching on her door. Emily Crowther entered carrying a bandbox in one hand and her reticule in the other.

"Have you put your socks in there?" Celia asked, eyeing the bandbox.

"Yes. And there is still space if you should like to add the others you have."

Emily placed the box on the bed, and Celia took off the lid. Inside were five pairs of beautifully knitted socks. "Oh, Emily," Celia exclaimed. "These are lovely; you do such even work."

Emily flushed at the praise. "I did a lot of knitting when I was younger, scarves for all my brothers. I have four—there are three younger than Todd at home. Actually, I think the quality of the wool has a lot to do with the finished product being so satisfactory. It is the finest I have ever seen."

Now it was Celia's turn to be pleased by the compliment. "When I next write my father, I will tell him what you said. It will delight him."

The two young women walked together along the lane to the village. The road beneath their feet was thick with leaves from the half-bare oak trees. Along the hedgerows the bramble leaves had turned dark red, with bright green veins standing out in sharp contrast. Overhead a thrush sang its sweet song. The day was cool and gray, but the wind was gentle and the stroll pleasant.

Their walk of just under a mile brought them to the rectory, a large, comfortable lodging of local stone. Beyond the rectory lay the churchyard, and beyond that the church with its tall bell tower.

As they went through the yard gate and down the path toward the house, a young boy of nine or ten came out the front door and walked toward them. He was tall and fair, and, Celia thought, quite a handsome young man. He was dressed as any other boy from the village, but when they met on the path, Celia was surprised to see that he did not act as most village boys would have. Instead of looking down or away and mumbling some indistinguishable greeting, this lad looked both Celia and Emily straight in the face and smiled as he said, "Good morning, ladies," and then "Excuse me" as he stepped off the path to let them go by.

Celia returned the greeting and the smile, then turned to look after him with interest as he walked to the gate and through it. When she turned back, Ursula was at the door to greet them.

"What a personable lad," Celia said. "Who is he?"

"Alan Drew," Ursula answered as she held the door wide for her guests to enter. They were shown into the parlor, a comfortable room with flowered carpets, flowered pillows, and flowered draperies. Nothing seemed to match, and yet all went together to create a warm, welcoming atmosphere.

"Alan Drew? Mrs. Drew's son? The one who lost his father?"

"Yes. He takes lessons from my father."

"What kind of lessons?"

"Reading and writing, mathematics, history."

Celia's expression showed her surprise, and Ursula continued. "He looks like one of the village boys, I know. But his mother was gently born, the daughter of the squire of the district."

"But Lord Wexford said the boy loves farming. How will his education benefit him as a farmer?"

"Wexford thinks he may have a future as an estate agent. For that occupation he'll need his studies and farm experience, too."

The rector joined them then, and Celia said no

more, but she was intrigued by the Drew boy who
had tragically lost his father but had apparently
found a patron in Lord Wexford.

Chapter 10

ON THE DAY of Lady Walsh's party, Ursula rode her horse over to the Priory in the afternoon and left him in the stables. Her dress and all she needed were carefully set aside in Celia's room. She savored a wonderfully hot bath (those she enjoyed at home were most often of the lukewarm variety).

Later, Wylie carefully arranged both girls' hair to their satisfaction. While they dressed, she flitted between the two, tying petticoat ribbons here, doing up hooks there, fastening the delicate clasps of jewelry, arranging a stray curl. When they were through, the maid was convinced that Ursula in her blue and Celia in her green would outshine all the other young ladies present that evening.

As they walked downstairs together before dinner, some of Ursula's earlier excitement faded.

"I feel like a hypocrite," she said.

"But why?"

"Because I always disparage gatherings like this, and here I am taking part in one."

"You of all people deserve some entertainment, Ursula. You give so much of your time to others. Why shouldn't you wear a lovely gown and dance the night away occasionally? It does no harm to enjoy oneself."

"Perhaps not, but some make a career of enjoying themselves, and for that there can be no excuse."

Celia and Ursula had been among the first to arrive in the drawing room, but within a few minutes John Hardy walked in. He was immaculate in a black evening coat and knee breeches, gray-striped waistcoat, and dazzling white linen. A single diamond sparkled within the folds of his intricately tied cravat. A large ruby glimmered on his left hand.

"By God, he's handsome," Ursula breathed. "How can a man be so handsome and yet have such a wicked tongue?"

"I think he takes you up because you give him the kind of verbal battle he most enjoys." Celia shifted her gaze from Mr. Hardy to Ursula and said shrewdly, "You admire him a little, don't you?"

Ursula let out what Mrs. Demming would have called an unladylike snort. "When I was ten, I was passionately in love with him. I used to daydream about us: that I would grow up, that he would suddenly notice me and fall madly in love with me. But that was before I knew I—"

"Before you knew what?"

"That was before I knew, before I understood what kind of man he is."

"And what kind of man is he?"

"He drinks, he gambles."

"But many gentlemen do the same."

"He keeps an expensive mistress and flaunts her before society."

"I think many gentlemen also indulge—"

"Don't make excuses for him, Celia. Just because many do it, that doesn't make it right. He will willingly seduce any woman foolish enough to fall victim to his charms. But when the time comes to marry, with his wealth and his high connections, he will wed only the brightest and the best London society has to offer."

Still in an effort to defend Mr. Hardy, a gentleman Celia had immediately taken a liking to, she said, "How do you know this about him?"

"I hear things."

"Rumors, you mean. I can't believe you listen to rumors. They may or may not be true."

"Whether it is true of him or not, I have seen ample evidence of the evil caused by such liaisons. Maggie, the little girl you read the story to that first day at the orphanage—her mother was a 'kept woman'—a gentleman's mistress. The child was an unwelcome complication, so she has no home now but the one we give her."

Their conversation was interrupted as Tony joined them and dinner was announced. As Celia took Tony's arm she pondered Ursula's remarks. She had always sensed the tension in the relationship between John and Ursula. She had never suspected the bitterness Ursula harbored for the gentleman. She wondered if Tony could confirm or deny the rumors Ursula had heard, but knew she could never raise such a subject with him.

The lavish three-course dinner passed without incident. Celia was seated between Lord Matlock and Trevor Farr and shared her time equally between the two gentlemen. Afterward the company was delighted when Lord Wexford came downstairs, said he would join his mother to greet their friends and neighbors, but declined to take any part in the festivities to follow. He was dressed as the other gentlemen in dark evening clothes. His cravat was perfection, and Celia suspected Mr. Hardy was once again responsible. She turned to Tony, who stood beside her. "Robert's color is much better, don't you think?"

"Definitely. He improves every day. His face is no longer so gaunt; he is finally gaining back some of the weight he lost."

"And his limp is less pronounced, I think."

"I agree. It warms my heart that he is willing to see people at last. Look at Mother. She's so delighted."

Lady Walsh did indeed look pleased to have Robert beside her. As the guests arrived in a steady stream, they exclaimed one and all over Lord Wexford's safe return. Then, as they were introduced to Celia, they exclaimed once again at Anthony's happy news and offered the couple felicitations.

Celia's meeting with the Duchess of Multree came rather early in the evening. Celia was standing between Robert and Tony when Tony made the introduction. The imposing matron scrutinized Celia from top to bottom before she said, "So you're the gel who tumbled down the stairs at Eugenia Rutledge's soiree?"

Fighting down her inevitable embarrassment at this blunt remark, Celia caught Tony's eye for quick encouragement and, remembering Robert's words, sank into a deep curtsy as she said very evenly, "Yes, Your Grace."

The old lady snorted. "You've backbone as well as beauty, I see. You'll do for Anthony, I have no doubt."

When she was gone, Robert leaned close to Celia and said, "You can stop worrying. She liked you."

Celia smiled, took a deep breath, and knew that with this hurdle behind her, she could relax and enjoy the evening.

When the last of the guests had straggled in, Robert took his departure. Seeing him leave unobtrusively, Celia hurried after him, catching up with him at the bottom of the stairway. "Must you go? Everyone would love it if you stayed."

"I'm tired," he said. "And I've created too much of a flurry already. It's your night; yours and Tony's."

"We are more than happy to share it with you."

"I know you are. You're a sweet child. But go now and enjoy yourself. Tomorrow you can tell me all about it."

Celia performed the opening waltz with Tony and felt light as air as he turned her gracefully in the dance. Later she took the floor with John Hardy, Trevor Farr, Lord Matlock, and she believed, each and every one of the gentlemen present. Every time she looked for Ursula she found her dancing, too, much sought after as a partner and glowing with a beautiful smile on her face.

At one point, watching Ursula waltz with Tony, she saw that John Hardy was watching them, too. She made her way to his side. She suspected that he had a high regard for Ursula, despite their constant fencing with words. She could not understand the almost angry look she saw now on his unguarded face.

"Something displeases you, Mr. Hardy," she said.

As soon as she spoke the look disappeared, to be replaced by his polite society mask. "Not at all, Miss Demming."

"Have you danced with Ursula tonight?"

"Not yet. She promised me a waltz after supper."

"My mother is always fond of saying that one can catch more flies with honey than with vinegar," she said rather cryptically.

He regarded her curiously for a moment before he replied, "But surely that is only true, Miss Demming, when the fly has not already been caught?"

Near midnight the guests wandered off by twos and threes to enjoy the fine supper laid out in the dining room. Later, when the band had resumed, John Hardy sought out Ursula to claim the dance she had promised him.

As they took the floor together, he said, "You are looking particularly lovely tonight. I like the way you've done your hair."

She looked up at him questioningly, as if she felt perhaps the compliment was not sincere, but she replied, "Thank you."

"It occurs to me," he continued, "that we have never danced together before." His hand moved at her waist and drew her a fraction closer.

"No, of course not," she replied. "There has never been an opportunity."

"There has been no opportunity because you have

always refused to come to these gatherings in the past. In fact, I was most certain you scorned them. Why did you come tonight?"

As always, her temper goaded by his inflammatory comments, she replied, "You can be certain it was not for the opportunity to add to my consequence by standing up with you."

"Ah, but you never know," he replied, unruffled. "Being noticed by me has been the making of more than one debutante, I promise you. Some say only Brummell's approval, in his day, carried more weight."

"What arrogance," she said, then missed her step. When he nearly trod upon her foot, she stopped dancing. "I'm sorry. I have had enough for one night. I cannot stay longer." And with nothing more than that, she turned and walked away leaving him in the middle of the dance floor.

For a moment he stood there in shock. Never in his life had a partner deserted him in the middle of a dance. Recovering quickly from his astonishment, he hurried after her, coming up with her in the deserted hall at the bottom of the stairs.

He caught her by the arm, and her momentum spun her around to face him. "What is it, Ursula? Where are you going?"

"I'm going upstairs to get out of this damnable dress. And then I am going home."

She pulled away from him and, lifting her skirts, hurried up the stairs. He stood watching her from the bottom of the stairway, but as soon as she disappeared from sight, he hurried after her again. She had gone to Celia's room, and he followed her there. She had left the door to the hallway standing half open. He pushed it wide. She turned to glare at him when he entered, but continued to undo the tiny hooks that fastened her dress at the front.

"Do you plan to undress here in front of me?" he challenged.

"You need not stay," she fired back. "And don't look so shocked. Tell me that you have never been in a lady's boudoir. I know it is the custom in London for men to be present while a lady is still in her underdress. Pretend that's what's happening here."

Finally free of the hooks, she stripped the gown from her shoulders and stepped out of it, then reached for her riding habit, which was lying on Celia's bed. She had pulled it on and buttoned several buttons before he stepped up to her and took her none too gently by the shoulders.

"You are acting quite mad, you know," he said. "What is it? Is it that Tony is so obviously in love? Must you admit at last that you can't have him?"

Then, before he could stop her, she pulled her right arm free from his grasp and slapped him across the face with her open palm. "How dare you?" she raged. "How dare you say such things? You don't know what you're talking about!"

"Oh, but I do. I know exactly how it feels to care for someone who is in love with someone else."

And then without permission or warning, he kissed her full upon the mouth, silencing whatever she would have said next.

For one fleeting moment the old daydream flashed through her mind: John realizing he loved her; John sealing that love with a kiss. His touch was so much more than she had imagined—full of fire, demanding, possessive.

Then as he crushed her body against his and the kiss deepened, she came to her senses. This was not the fulfillment of a girlhood dream. This was John Hardy, practiced flirt and seducer. This was no kiss of love; this was a kiss of desire. She pushed him away, and when she looked up into his face she saw that she had hurt him, for his cheek was bright red where she had slapped it. "Don't trifle with me, John. I am not one of your flirts. I cannot be what you want me to be."

She snatched up her cloak and pushed past him without another word. Making her way through the corridors toward the back of the house, Ursula hurried down a secondary stair to the kitchens. She had gone all the way to the stables before she realized that she had come away in her flimsy dancing slippers and left her riding boots behind. She ordered her horse saddled anyway and ignored the groom's astonished face when he took her foot in his hand to put her up. She turned her horse into the shadowy lane and allowed him to pick his way home through the darkness.

Shortly before one o'clock, Celia noticed Ursula's absence. When she asked if anyone knew where she was, Emily said she had seen her go upstairs earlier after leaving John Hardy in the middle of a dance. Thinking Ursula might be ill, Celia excused herself and hurried upstairs. In her room she found Ursula's dress on the floor, but no sign of Ursula.

When she returned to the party, Tony asked, "Did you find her?"

"No. I think she may have gone home."

"John is gone, too. I haven't seen him since before supper."

"Do you think they could be together?"

"Possibly. If she went home, perhaps he escorted her."

"She would be safe with him, Tony, wouldn't she?" When he looked puzzled at her question, she went on. "What I mean is . . . he wouldn't do anything . . . improper . . . or inappropriate?"

He frowned as if he considered the question ridiculous. "No. He would not. He is a gentleman, first and last."

While Celia and Anthony were having this discussion, John Hardy was in his room, lying on top of his bed fully clothed with his hands folded behind his head, staring at the shadows cast by his fire upon the ceiling. In her room at the rectory, Ursula was also in bed, sobbing quietly into her pillows.

Chapter 11

IT WAS NEARLY three o'clock in the morning when Celia finally went to sleep. She was worried by Ursula's sudden and unexplained departure, especially when she saw the riding boots that had been left behind. The same day before noon, she walked to the rectory to speak with Ursula herself. When she arrived there, Mrs. Browne told her that Ursula had gone riding, and she had no idea when she might return.

Disappointed, Celia left a note for her friend, telling her that she had called and that she needed to speak with her. When she arrived back at the Priory, she encountered Leech in the great hall. "Have you seen Mr. Graydon, Leech?"

"He's gone shooting, miss, with the other gentlemen."

"Of course, they've gone. The weather is good." It had rained almost continuously for the three days preceding the party, keeping the men at home. She should have guessed that they would be anxious to be gone now that the skies had cleared. "Is Lord Wexford downstairs?"

"He is in the salon, miss."

141

Knowing that none of the other ladies would be down for some time yet, Celia went to the morning room to collect her knitting, then crossed to the salon. She had slept through her regularly appointed time with Wexford, perhaps there was something she could do for him now.

When she came into the room, he was sitting in an armchair near the fire with his head leaning back and his eyes closed. Thinking he was asleep, she turned to go away again, but before she took even one step, he lifted his head and turned to face her.

"Who is it?"

"Celia. I'm sorry if I disturbed you."

"You're not disturbing me. Please, come in."

"The sun is shining for the first day in four," she said. "How should you like a walk in the gardens, with me as your guide?"

"The walk sounds excellent. My leg needs exercise. But let's make it the maze, and *I* will be *your* guide."

"All right, but I warn you I don't know my way out, so if we get lost, it will all be on your head."

One of the footmen was sent running for Wexford's coat and her pelisse, and they were soon on their way. They left the house by the front door, then circled around the south side toward the rear. Once past the kitchen gardens, they let themselves through a wrought-iron gate in the stone wall surrounding the formal gardens to the west of the house. They slowly traversed several paths, ascended two shallow flights of stairs, and finally arrived at the entrance to the maze. Facing the wall of carefully clipped hedge, which extended a considerable distance in both directions, Celia said, "We are at the entrance. Now what?"

"Take us wherever you like. When we want to leave, I can tell you the way out."

She regarded him skeptically. "How will you be able to do that?"

"Trust me, Celia," he challenged.

"Very well, I will trust you. But tell me this: Why do I have the feeling that come dinnertime, we will be lost, and the entire household will be searching for us?"

"You have that feeling because you don't trust me."

She glanced up at his face and saw that he was laughing at her. In the strong daylight she observed that the dark circles that had persisted beneath his eyes were now completely gone.

Taking his arm she led off boldly through the maze opening, turning left, then right, back and forth until she was hopelessly lost. Eventually they came to an arbor. It had been covered with vining roses that were dying, but it had a solid roof and a comfortable bench fitted with soft cushions.

"We have come to a lovely arbor," she said. "Shall we sit?"

"Why not?"

She led him to the bench, then sat beside him and immediately took her knitting from the bag she carried on the opposite arm. When he heard the needles clicking, he reached over toward the sound, encountering the soft wool of an almost finished sock.

"What are you making?"

"Another sock for the orphanage."

"Is this your father's wool? It feels amazingly soft."

"It is fine, isn't it?" she agreed. "Emily . . . Emily Crowther is so skillful. You should see the beautiful work she does with it."

"I should arrange to have some of this wool sent to Pierre," he said.

"The man you stayed with in Belgium?"

"Yes. Did I tell you he was a weaver?"

"No, I don't think so."

"Well, he is. And I think he is probably a good one, but the raw material he has to work with is of such inferior quality that he gets very little for the goods he produces. With wool like this, he could do much better."

"Have you had any news of him since he brought you home?"

"No. But I didn't expect to. He can't write. And it won't do me any good to write to him, either, for he can't read."

"We could certainly arrange to send him some wool," Celia said. "We can send a letter along, and I am sure that the village minister, or priest or whoever, could read it to him."

"I would like that. I have always wanted to repay him, but could never hit upon a way."

"It's important to you. To pay debts."

"Yes. Though sometimes it's not possible."

"Where exactly did you say Pierre lives?"

"On the eastern edge of Louvain."

"And what is his surname?"

"Amay. Pierre Amay."

"I'll write to my father tomorrow, and we'll see what can be done."

"You haven't told me about the party last night."

She smiled, remembering. "The food was delicious, the music heavenly, the company wonderfully agreeable—and Tony was most attentive."

"In other words, you enjoyed yourself."

"Yes, I did, except for . . ."

"Except for what?"

"Ursula left early, without explaining why. I went to call on her this morning, but she wasn't home. I admit I am a bit worried about her."

"You must know that last night's assembly was not one of Ursula's favorite places to be. No doubt she left when she felt she'd had enough."

Celia nodded her agreement. "I thought that, too, and perhaps you're right. But I will feel better when I have had a chance to talk with her."

"I'm sure you will see her tonight, and she will explain all. But tell me, what did you wear last night?"

"My gown was mint green, a color Tony especially likes with my hair. It had Brussels lace around the hem and overlaying the sleeves. I wore the pearls my father gave me for my eighteenth birthday, and Tony's ring, of course."

"I wish I could have seen you," he said. Then, with a touch of frustration, he added, "I wish I *could* see you."

Celia laid her knitting aside and turned toward him on the bench. "You will see me. Someday soon. I'm sure of it."

"You say your hair is dark with touches of red?"

"Yes."

"How do you wear it?"

"Most often like I have it now. Feel it. I don't mind."

He accepted her offer. As he carefully reached toward where he thought her hair would be, she took his hand and placed it on her shining curls.

"It's so soft, like the hair of an angel."

She laughed. "And when have you ever felt the hair of an angel, my lord?"

He chuckled as well. "Never." He had brought his second hand to the opposite side of her head and now lowered both hands to her shoulders. "And tell me about your neck, Miss Demming. Is it the neck of a swan?"

"Decide for yourself, sir."

He raised his hands, one to each side of her neck, and she shivered at his touch. "Are you cold?" he asked.

"No. You're tickling me!"

"I'm sorry, but now I must know about the nose and chin, surely the most formidable aspects of any Briton." His hands traced the sides of her neck to her chin. "Strong, without question formidable. Cheeks are round, soft." He smiled. "Probably rosy. Forehead is broad and intelligent; brows, delicately arched; eyes, closed; lashes very long and soft. Ah! The nose, patrician—perfect. And the lips . . ." Her lips parted as his fingers brushed them, and he felt her shallow, quickened breath. "The lips . . . are entirely kissable." His hands moved to cup her face, and he lowered his own mouth to hers.

When he touched her neck, Celia shivered. When his fingers came to her eyes, she closed them. By the time he brushed her lips, she was struggling for breath. By the time he kissed her, she was unable to think clearly. Celia gasped as his mouth took hers. His soft, mesmerizing words had clouded her brain. His lips, hungry and searching, made her go limp. She felt his arms reach around to steady her, felt him pull her close, felt her own lips offering themselves to him . . . and then suddenly she was on her feet, backing away from him, her eyes brimming, then overflowing with tears. She raised both hands to her mouth to cover it, trying to hold back the sobs she felt rising in her throat.

When she broke away so suddenly, his arms followed her. When she was beyond his reach, he slowly lowered them.

"Celia?" His only answer was her muffled sob from somewhere in the void before him.

Then, as she watched, he dropped his head into his hands as if he had a sudden and violent headache. "Oh, my God, what have I done?"

She turned suddenly and started to walk away. "Celia!" he called. "Don't leave. You'll get lost. Celia!"

Even as flustered as she was his words registered, and she stopped after she had turned only one corner.

Not knowing she had stopped, he shouted after her, "Go west, toward the sun, or right when you have a choice. Do you hear me? Only west or right."

She heard, and she needed to hear no more. She walked straight to the first cross path and turned toward the sun. Her next choice was right, then right again, then west. Often she walked for some distance in what she was convinced was the wrong direction, but she stuck to the rule of west or right and discovered that the key to the maze was perfect: In a reasonable space of time, she found herself at the entrance. It was only when she arrived there that she realized she had stranded Lord Wexford within.

She decided she would find one of the gardeners and send him to fetch Lord Wexford, then wondered how she would explain having left him alone in the first place. Undecided what to do, she sat on a bench inside the entrance and struggled to calm herself.

Wexford sat where she had left him, with no thought at all for the maze or his inability to find his way out alone. Trying to take in what had happened, the only solution he could discover that was remotely acceptable was that he had gone completely mad. To have taken advantage of such a young girl while they were quite alone, and she was for the moment under his protection, was bad enough. But to have kissed a young woman who was promised to another, and, in fact, promised to his own brother, bordered on the insane.

He tried to recall moment by moment what had transpired. He knew his original intent was to let his hands feel her features so that he could in some sense "see" her. Yet somewhere in the midst of that "seeing," his general interest had become very personal. The softness of her hair and the faint scent of lavender that rose from her drove other thoughts from his mind. When he felt her parted lips and quickened breathing, he forgot who he was and who she was and followed the instinct that demanded a kiss.

Now he knew he had done irreparable harm. Her reaction showed that clearly enough. He had driven a wedge between them, into the very heart of the strong bond of friendship they had formed over the past weeks.

After sitting for some moments in confused thought, Celia rose and hurried back into the maze. The last thing in the world she wanted to do was face Lord Wexford again, but she knew she could not leave him alone. She also knew she could not explain to the servants why she had deserted him. She must go herself.

Not at all convinced she could even find the arbor again, or that he would still be there if she did, she hurried down the paths. She tried reversing the pattern—east or left—but it didn't work. Finally, by sheer good fortune, she rounded a corner and the arbor stood before her. Wexford sat exactly where she had left him; her knitting lay on the ground near his feet.

He must have heard her coming, for when she stopped he looked in her direction, but he did not speak.

In her most formal voice, one that made his heart sink, she said, "I have come to lead you from the maze, but you must promise me first that there will be no repetition of . . . that you will not . . ."

He nodded and stood. "I promise. But Celia, we must talk about this. You must let me apologize."

She walked nearer and collected her knitting. As she took his arm and turned him toward the path, she said, "I don't want to talk about it. I don't even want to think about it. And I don't think there is any apology you could make that I would find acceptable."

Seeing that she was even more angry than he feared, he said, "I was hoping to plead insanity, for I, too, could think of no other excuse you might believe."

At each new path Celia consulted the sun, turning west or right as the opportunities presented themselves. She was making the best speed she dared leading a blind man with a pronounced limp.

Without pausing in her businesslike march through the maze, she replied, "To be fair, I must take some responsibility. My mother taught me better, and I have not heeded her lessons as I should. I know I should never be alone in a secluded place with a man not related. My behavior in coming here alone with you no doubt led you to believe you could take liberties—"

"What utter rubbish! Don't you dare mouth such nonsense to me. You are my brother's intended wife, and there was *nothing* inappropriate in your behavior. The fault was all mine, and I take full responsibility." Then, with a sincerity in his voice that she almost believed, he said, "You must know, Celia, that I would never do anything to hurt you."

"But that's just the problem, don't you see? You already have."

Knowing this to be the indisputable truth, he remained silent for the balance of their walk back to the house. When she left him at the foot of the stairs, he wanted to shout after her, ask her if she intended to tell Tony what had happened. But he did not, for he knew that whatever she decided to do, he had no power to influence her.

Celia joined the other ladies in the sitting room briefly to say she had been walking with Lord Wexford but now had the headache and would like to retire for a few hours to her room.

"It's all that dancing till the small hours," Lady Aylesbury offered. "Puts a person off their rhythm, and sometimes it takes a few days to feel just so again."

Lady Walsh added, "And if you aren't feeling better by dinnertime, Celia, don't feel you must come down. Cook can send up a tray whenever you like."

Thanking them for their kindness, Celia retreated to the safety of her room. She knew she needed time, considerable time, to digest what had happened and decide what, if anything, she could do about it.

Her first question was why. Why had he kissed her? Despite his words to the contrary, she still felt she carried some part of the blame. She had, after all, invited him to feel her hair, even laughingly permitted his further exploration. She had *not*, however, invited the kiss . . . or had she? Perhaps she should have pulled away sooner, after he touched her eyes, or before he touched her lips, before her breath grew shallow and painful and her senses dull.

She could find no answers. It had happened. It could not be undone. If it had been any other man, perhaps she could have shrugged it off as a whim of passion, a momentary temptation. A man stealing a kiss was surely nothing new. But this man was Tony's brother. She had trusted him. Now she no longer felt she could.

This thinking brought her to her second question. Should she tell Tony what Robert had done? She knew she would hurt them both if she did. But she also knew that her relationship with Robert must now change. How could she explain this change to Tony without telling him the reason for it?

She knew she could no longer go to the book room and sit alone with Robert as she had in the past. But what explanation could she give Tony for not going? And she knew that in the future, after she and Tony were wed, it would be uncomfortable to meet Robert when they would know what had passed between them while Tony would remain in ignorance.

She couldn't see a solution, and her anger burned at Robert for placing her in this situation. What right had he had to take her rosy world and turn it gray?

The afternoon faded to evening, and Celia still kept to her room. Tony spoke with her briefly after dinner, and she was grateful for the opportunity to tell him how much she had enjoyed the party.

"I feel guilty about not coming down this evening," she said.

"Don't. You are not the only deserter. Lady Matlock retired directly after dinner claiming fatigue, Ursula never came tonight, and John has gone off to Robert's room."

"Did you see Ursula at all today?" she asked. "I'm still worried about her."

"No, I haven't seen her, but I'm sure she's fine. No doubt she will be over tomorrow at the regular time to collect you for the orphanage."

Admitting that he was undoubtedly right, Celia said good night, and Tony went off to the billiards room where Trevor Farr and Lord Matlock awaited him. Celia rang for Wylie and prepared for bed, wishing that there was someone, anyone in whom she could confide. She had always felt that Tony would be a wonderful confidant. Then, the first time she needed him, the subject was one she could not share.

While Celia sat and worried alone, John Hardy had taken a bottle of brandy to his cousin's bedchamber. The two men settled comfortably near the fire, the bottle on a table between them. John was only a year younger than Robert. Possessed of similar temperaments and sharing similar interests, they had always been close. They spoke of politics and acquaintances; they remembered lost friends. And though neither was the type to share amorous exploits, John seemed of a mind to do so tonight. Like Celia, he had spent much time with his own thoughts. Now he felt he needed to consult a friend.

"I made a fool of myself at your mother's little gathering last night."

Robert replied ruefully, "It must be something in the air."

"Why do you say that?"

Wexford brushed the question aside. "Never mind, it's not important. What foolish thing did you do?"

"I kissed Ursula Browne."

At Wexford's immediate frown, John replied, "I know you warned me off her years ago. I thought then it was because you knew she cared for Tony. Idiot that I am, I thought that now Tony is spoken for, she might look my way."

"I didn't warn you off because of Tony. I think it's highly unlikely that Ursula has any romantic interest in him."

John frowned, regarding his cousin intently. "Then it's you she is in love with."

Wexford looked even more startled at this pronouncement. "No. She's not. She cares for us both, it's true, but not in the way you mean."

"I'm not sure I agree with you, but of one thing I am certain. She has no time for me, and never has had."

"Can you blame her? You ruffle her feathers at every opportunity!"

"And she gives as good as she gets," John fired back.

Wexford had to agree. "You're right. No doubt you would suit perfectly."

"Why did you warn me off two years ago?"

"Because there are things about Ursula that you don't know."

"Such as?"

"I am not at liberty to say. Let me say only that even if she did return your regard, there would be obstacles—serious obstacles."

"You're sounding very mysterious."

"I don't mean to. I only want you to know that I did not interfere initially for any frivolous reason. I was concerned for your well-being, and for Ursula's, too."

"You know her as well as anyone," John continued. "Would she enumerate these 'obstacles' you speak of, if I forced the issue?"

"I can't answer that. I don't know how she feels about you."

"Nor do I."

"Did she say anything when you kissed her?" Wexford asked.

"Only that she would not be one of my flirts."

"Is that what you want her to be?"

John scowled at his cousin and said sarcastically, "What high regard you hold me in, to be sure. I wish you could see my face. . . . No! I am not interested in Miss Browne as my latest flirt."

"Then, perhaps, the first thing you should do is explain the precise role you wish her to fill, so that there can be no misunderstanding as to your intentions."

They spoke no more of Ursula that evening, but John sought his bed some hours later in a contemplative mood. His cousin had given him much to think on.

After John had left him, Wexford retired to bed but had trouble sleeping. He thought it unfortunate that John's fancy should have settled upon Ursula, but he knew better than most how difficult it was to predict to whom one would be attracted.

During the hours that had passed since he had

kissed Celia, he had admitted to himself that he was enchanted by her. And he also knew that those feelings, newborn and strong, must be buried forever, both for the love he bore his brother and for the future harmony of his family.

Chapter 12

CELIA SPENT AN impossible night. Much of the time she sat up, trying to understand the situation she had gotten herself into. Sometimes she napped, only to wake again feeling unsettled and unrested. She had many conflicting emotions, and she didn't know which ones were real, which ones she could trust. She went back to the beginning and relived her moments with Tony. She reviewed again in her memory her conversations with Robert.

Try as she might, she could not put Robert's kiss from her mind. Tony's kisses had always excited her; Robert's kiss had turned her world wrong side up. With very little effort she could recall the way he held her, the way his mouth had felt pressed hungrily to hers. At one point, waking from sleep, she actually felt she was in his arms. She wanted him to go on kissing her, never to stop.

In the harshness of the dawn, she felt she must be what the world considered a wanton woman. To desire two men simultaneously must be a sin.

She thought finally she had come face-to-face with love—with that one word that encompassed so much that poets had struggled for centuries to define it.

She knew now that it was indefinable because it was different for everyone. She loved Tony. But if she loved Tony, why was she so strongly drawn to Wexford? She had to admit she *was* drawn to him, although she couldn't understand why, for Tony was everything a woman could ask for in a man.

She dressed very early, without summoning Wylie, in a simple blue morning gown. Then she wrote a short note, folded it, and went quietly down the hall to slip it under Tony's door. She asked him to join her in the drawing room as soon as possible, for she needed to speak with him in private.

She then went to the drawing room, where she knew she would be undisturbed this early in the day. A footman in the hallway opened the door for her and stopped to stir the bed of banked coals and add a few logs before he left her alone. She sat near the hearth, watching the fire spring to life.

She rose when Tony entered, and he came to take her hands as he asked, "Have you been waiting long?"

"Not quite an hour."

"I only saw your note a few minutes ago. Why didn't you knock, or send someone for me?"

"It's all right. I didn't mind waiting."

He regarded her tired face with concern and led her to a sofa near the warmth of the fire. After adding more logs, he sat beside her. "You look very tired," he said. "Aren't you sleeping well?"

"I hardly slept at all last night."

"Are you ill? Shall I send for the doctor?"

"No, Tony. I'm not ill. I'm troubled. That's why I need to talk with you.'"

"What is it? What's troubling you?"

She took a deep breath and let it out but still didn't speak. He remained silent, deep concern evident in his face.

"I don't know how to say this," she began. "I don't think there is a proper way, or an easy way, or any way to do it without hurting you."

He took both her hands in his, holding them in a warm reassuring clasp. "Please, tell me."

"I can't . . . I can't marry you." As she watched his brows draw together in disbelief, she hurried on. "It's not that I don't love you. I do. But I think the problem is that I am not *in love* with you, and I don't know how to make myself be, or even if it's possible."

Trying to take in this confused speech, he said, "Is this what's been on your mind, yesterday and last night?"

When she nodded, he put an arm around her shoulders and pulled her against him. He didn't speak, and Celia, too, remained silent. After some time had passed, he asked, "Are you quite sure?"

When she only nodded mutely, he tipped her face up with his hand to make her look at him. "You should have come to me when you first had doubts, instead of making yourself sick with worry."

"I couldn't, for I had to think things through. It took me some time, for I have been very confused. Some things, though, I have sorted out, and I want to tell you, so that you will understand how I have come to this decision.

"From as early as I can remember, my goal in life

was to marry well. It was all my mother cared about. Having five daughters was quite daunting for my parents, I think, and they were determined to see us all suitably established. I didn't care much for most of the men my mother thought would be a good match for me. But that first night I saw you, I thought you were wonderfully handsome. I was so flattered by your attention. But when I look back now, I can see that it was the idea of marriage that I was enamored of, the chance of marrying better than my sisters.

"What I did was wrong, sinfully wrong, for I led you to believe I had feelings I never had."

"You never said you loved me," he said.

She smiled sadly, finding it interesting that he had noticed that omission. "Nor did you ever say it to me. Perhaps that fact is more revealing than anything we have said so far."

He kissed her then, a sweet, sentimental kiss that she suspected would be the last she ever received from him. She felt one moment of chilling panic. What if she was wrong and was throwing away her one chance at happiness?

When the kiss ended, she felt the tears standing in her eyes and struggled to hold them back. "You've taught me so much, Tony, in these past weeks. You've given me the courage to stand on my own, make my own decisions. For that, and for so much more, I will always love you. It breaks my heart that I can't love you the way you want me to."

"We'll talk again," he said, "but if you don't mind,

I'd like some time alone to think about all you've said."

She nodded and started to leave the room. As she reached the door, his voice stayed her. "Celia, thank you for being honest with me. I know it was difficult for you."

She smiled thinly, then left without speaking. Back in her room she sat and wrote to her father, telling him to expect her home in a few days. As soon as Lady Walsh was informed of her change in status, Celia would send down for her trunks and put her mind to the business of packing.

When the appointed hour came for Celia to meet with Wexford, she stayed in her room, but she couldn't get him off her mind. She had come to look forward to the time she spent with him, even though he was often moody and sometimes cross. She wondered who would read to him now, or indeed, if anyone would. At least now that she was leaving, she wouldn't have to explain to Tony why she no longer met with his brother.

She was waiting when Ursula called in the early afternoon to collect her for their scheduled trip to the orphanage. She felt a pang of guilt at leaving her work there. There was much she wanted to do that would now be left undone. She had barely started her lessons with Kitty, and the child had so much to learn. Celia felt guilty about asking Ursula to take on this task when she already had so much to do.

Celia's first words as they rode off together were

of the party. "I was worried when you left the other night without saying good-bye."

"I was tired," Ursula replied simply. "I am not accustomed to such activity and such late hours. I should have found you to say good night. I'm sorry."

Her tone was clipped and formal, and Celia felt she was not hearing the whole story. This explanation didn't reveal why Ursula had left her boots behind, or why she had felt it necessary to leave her partner in the middle of a dance.

"Ursula, there is something I need to tell you. It's not common knowledge yet, but I know I can trust you to keep it to yourself until Tony has told Lady Walsh. I have broken my engagement; I will be leaving Walsh Priory in a few days."

Ursula pulled her horse up and turned to look at Celia in astonishment.

"I know you're surprised," Celia said. "I'm still rather in shock myself, but I believe it is the right thing to do."

"But Tony loves you so. He will be devastated."

"I think in time he will come to see that although we are very fond of each other, and in many ways well suited, we were not meant to be together."

As they rode on, Ursula lapsed into silence until Celia spoke again. "I regret more than I can say that I must leave my work with you at the orphanage. I have enjoyed it so much."

"The children will miss you. I will miss you."

"I will write, and perhaps sometime you can come to Yorkshire to visit me. And I want you to let me know when Mrs. Forbes runs low on cloth. I will send more whenever you need it."

"Don't you need to see her today?" Ursula asked as they rode into the village.

"Yes, I do. I have the measurements for a coat for Willy and a dress for little Virginia."

"I must stop at the smithy," Ursula replied. "My horse has a loose shoe. I'll come back for you."

Ursula rode on as Celia dismounted outside Mrs. Forbes's cottage and tied her horse to a gnarled apple tree beside the path.

The cottage was of moderate size, solidly constructed of Chiltern flint. Celia found Mrs. Forbes expecting her. There was hot water for tea on the hob and fresh biscuits on the sturdy hand-hewn table.

Mrs. Forbes was plump and rosy; Celia had never seen her without a smile on her face. She knew everything that went on in the village and was an excellent source of information. If someone was ailing, if a new babe had been born or a cow lost, she always seemed one of the first to know.

"Sit you down, Miss Demming, and I'll pour you a hot cup of tea after your chilling ride." Although the ride had not been long, the day was cold and the warmth of the cottage welcoming. Celia wrapped her icy fingers around the steaming teacup Mrs. Forbes set before her.

"I have a coat here for you, miss, all finished."

She set a carefully stitched wool jacket on the table near Celia, and Celia handed her several coins. "You do such beautiful work, Mrs. Forbes. Sally will be delighted with this." The woman beamed at the praise, and Celia took a scrap of paper from her pocket. "I have the measurements for another coat and a dress."

Mrs. Forbes dropped the coins in a small clay pot on her fireplace mantel then took the piece of paper and perused it carefully. She could read enough to write her name and had learned to cipher some in order to make clothes to measure.

At that moment someone knocked on the door, and Mrs. Forbes went to answer it. Alan Drew stood outside. Mrs. Forbes hurried him in to close the door against the cold.

Alan smiled and greeted Celia, then handed Mrs. Forbes some mending that he said Mrs. Browne had asked him to drop off on his way past her cottage.

When he was gone, Celia said, "What a good-looking boy."

"Aye, he takes after his father and no mistake."

"I didn't know Mr. Drew. Was he a handsome man?"

"Lord love you, miss. There's not a soul in the village what believes that boy was sired by George Drew. He's the image of young Lord Wexford about the eyes. Sounds like him, too, if you've got a sharp ear."

"Lord Wexford is Alan Drew's father?"

There was so much shock in Celia's voice that Mrs. Forbes refilled her teacup and prepared to calm her ruffled sensibilities. "He couldn't a been no more than nineteen or so at the time, miss, and young lords are known to be wild in their salad days."

"But Miss Browne told me that Mrs. Drew was

gently born. Surely Lord Wexford would have married her if he was responsible for her . . . situation."

"Gentle born, yes, but no proper match for a viscount. She was the squire's daughter, his only child and such a beautiful girl, with all that long dark hair hangin' past her waist. I remember seein' her in Lord Wexford's company often in them days. And I remember, too, her sudden marriage to a man no one had ever heared of—from Norfolk I think he was. The babe arrived about seven months after, but big and strong and like no early baby I ever seen."

Through the tiny window facing the street, Celia could see Ursula trotting her horse down the road toward the cottage. She rose from the table, collected the coat, and thanked Mrs. Forbes for her efforts.

"Thank you, Miss Demming. It's pleased I am to have the steady work."

Celia and Ursula rode on to the orphanage together and found plenty there to occupy them. It wasn't until much later in the day that Celia had leisure to think about all Mrs. Forbes had said.

She found it hard to credit that Wexford would compromise a young girl and then refuse to marry her, but she had to admit that it all made sense. She had heard firsthand Wexford's reaction to the idea of the boy working in the quarry, and she suspected that it was Wexford who paid young Alan's tutoring fees. She had seen the rent roll and knew that the widow paid no rent. Celia also knew that Wexford made regular visits to the Drew cottage.

Had he renewed his relationship with Mrs. Drew now that her husband was gone?

After all the hours they had spent together, Celia felt she had come to know Wexford fairly well. Faced with his behavior in the maze and the revealing information from Mrs. Forbes, she realized that she had been naive.

Before dinner Tony and Celia talked again. He told her he had already spoken to his mother and that he would send the necessary notices to the newspaper. Celia shuddered to think what her mother would say when she read such tidings, but there was nothing she could do to prevent it. Lavinia was still in Hereford with Sophia, but Celia found that she didn't have the courage to write to her mother herself.

"Would it be possible not to say anything to the others until after I have gone?" she asked Tony. "I don't think I could face all their questions."

"When are you leaving?"

"I thought the day after tomorrow, if it's not inconvenient."

"Must you go so soon?"

"It wouldn't be right for me to stay, not under the circumstances."

"We'll tell everyone tonight that you're going home to Yorkshire, but we won't tell them why. That will give you the opportunity to say good-bye. After you have gone, I'll tell them that we decided we would not suit . . . if you're sure this is what you want?"

Hearing the hope in his voice, she said as gently as she could, "I'm sure. Very sure."

"I'll let the coachman know. What time?"

"Nine o'clock?"

"I'll be escorting you, of course."

"You needn't come, Tony; it's not necessary."

"I won't hear of you traveling all that distance alone. I intend to see you to your father's door, every single step of the way."

"Thank you. I will appreciate having your escort."

She had not relished the idea of traversing half the country with only Wylie and Lord Walsh's servants in attendance. She knew her mother would never approve of such an arrangement, but she had not dared to hope that Tony would be willing to accompany her. He was, without doubt, the most honorable gentleman she had ever known.

The following day was almost entirely consumed by Celia's departure plans. She had tied up as many loose ends as she could. Ursula and Leech would work together to see that Mrs. Forbes was kept busy with wool cloth and measurements. Emily Crowther, whose home was only three miles the other side of the orphanage, had offered to take over for Celia in teaching Kitty to read and write. She had also agreed to keep knitting socks, so long as there was a need.

On her final evening Celia said good-bye to everyone at dinner, saying, most truthfully, that she hoped to see them all again very soon. No one seemed eager for cards or charades; instead they sat talking of the coming holidays and of hunting and of the London Season that would start soon afterward.

In the midst of Lord Matlock's recounting of a hunt story involving a particularly clever fox, the door opened and Lord Wexford entered. He stopped just inside the door as all attention turned toward him.

"Excuse me for interrupting, but I was wondering, Miss Demming, if you could step up to the book room for a few minutes. There are several things I need to be clear on before you leave in the morning. It will take only a moment or two, I promise."

She knew instantly what he was doing, approaching her in public so there was no way she could refuse him without appearing uncivil. She forced a smile to her face, hoped it looked genuine, and said pleasantly, "Of course, Lord Wexford, I would be happy to."

Celia had cause to be thankful when Lady Walsh then added, "Perhaps it would be best, my dear, if you retired after you have finished with Wexford. You have an early start and a very long day tomorrow."

"Yes indeed. I think I shall. Good night, everyone."

After another round of good nights and good-byes, Celia left the room with Wexford. No sooner had the door closed and the footman moved out of earshot than she said very quietly, "How dare you? You must know I have no wish either to see you or speak with you." They started up the stairs; she offered him no assistance.

"Tony told me before dinner," he said, "that your engagement is ended, that you had decided you wouldn't suit. Obviously I had to speak with you. I apologize for my method, but I knew you would not come if I sent for you."

"How astute you are, sir."

"Celia, please. We need to talk about this. It is clear to me from what Tony said that you didn't tell him what happened between us."

"How could I tell him? You know how it would hurt him."

They had arrived at the book room door. She opened it and walked inside. She resisted the impulse to guide him as he reached for the frame to feel his way and followed her. He closed the door firmly.

"Hurt him?" he said. "Don't you think breaking the engagement has hurt him? He loves you. You love him. Don't throw that away."

"None of this is any of your concern, Lord Wexford. What Tony and I decide—"

"Of course it's my concern. It was my behavior that precipitated this hobble, wasn't it? Or has something else happened that I know nothing of?"

"No, there is nothing else," she said quietly.

He took an impulsive step toward her, reaching out to her as he did so. She took a step back, staying beyond his reach. "Celia, we can get past this. Don't throw it all away because of one impulsive kiss." He folded his hands together and gripped them till the knuckles showed white. "I don't know why I did it. It didn't mean *anything*, I swear. Tell

169

Tony, or don't tell him, or I'll tell him if you like, but don't leave him because of me."

She had always suspected that the kiss that had warmed her to the soul had been a commonplace act for him. But actually hearing him say the kiss had meant nothing hurt her even more.

His behavior and her reaction in the arbor that day had shown her that her feelings for Tony were not what they should have been, but she was not of a mind to thank Wexford for this lesson in love. She was now, thanks to him, unengaged, most likely to be the talk of the town again when the news broke. She would go home with no matrimonial prospects, to a mother who would most likely be ready to flay her alive for her behavior. She had no more time to waste worrying about the sensibilities of this man who had single-handedly unraveled her world.

She walked quickly to the door. "I must go now, Lord Wexford. There is nothing more to say."

She expected him to reply, to try to stop her, but he did neither. He stood still where she had left him, and he said nothing as she left the room.

Chapter 13

TWO DAYS LATER in the late afternoon, Anthony handed a weary Celia down from the traveling carriage. He had ridden the first day on horseback to avoid any awkwardness for her. When it started to snow, however, on the second morning, he gave in to Celia's entreaties to ride inside. Wylie sat opposite them, often nodding to sleep, and they talked amiably for many miles. It seemed to Celia that they would manage to remain friends.

As she stepped from the coach before the only home she had ever known, she looked up at the brick walls, and inexplicable tears came to her eyes. She felt as if she had been gone a very long time, as though she was not at all the same person who had left home only a few months ago to sample the Little Season. She felt years older.

Mr. Demming, tall and broad-shouldered with a smiling face, had been watching for them and met his youngest child in the front hall with his arms outspread. He knew from her letter that his girl was troubled.

When Celia emerged from her father's embrace, Mr. Demming shook hands with Anthony, saying how good it was to see him again. Over tea the couple explained the termination of their engagement. They felt they would not suit. Anthony hoped Mr. Demming would understand.

"I understand that you both seem to know your own minds, and it's not my place to interfere. If this is what you think is best, then so be it."

"I'm certain that Mrs. Demming will be disappointed," Anthony said.

"She is still in Hereford for Sophia's lying-in, but when she comes home, I will make sure that she understands. I won't allow her to tease Celia unnecessarily about it, you can depend upon that."

Anthony smiled and was reassured. He had a strong suspicion that Mrs. Demming would be very angry at her daughter. He wanted to shield Celia from that if he could.

Anthony declined his host's hospitality for the night, saying he could cover a goodly distance of his return journey if he left soon. After he had said good-bye to Mr. Demming in the salon, Celia walked with him to the front door. The butler, who had been standing in the hall, suddenly seemed to recall some business in another part of the house. He walked away, leaving them alone.

Tony took her hands and regarded her with a sad but resigned smile. "I suppose this is good-bye. I will never forget you, Celia, nor these months we've had together."

"I won't forget you, either, Tony. Not ever."

He raised her hand to his lips and kissed it gallantly, then collected his hat, gloves, and coat from the hall table, opened the door, and walked swiftly down the steps to the waiting coach. He turned at the door, smiled a brief farewell, then climbed inside. The coach rolled away.

Celia stood by the open door, the blustery air rushing in on her. When the coach door closed, she swung the big front door shut against the wintry blast. Her heart felt as cold as the December wind. Tony was walking out of her life. The kindest, gentlest man she had ever known, and she had sent him away. No doubt she was a fool. Then, as the salon door opened behind her, she turned to see her father standing there, tall, solid, always her port in a storm. Once again he held out his arms to her as her face dissolved in tears.

On the same afternoon that Tony was driving back from Yorkshire, John Hardy called at the rectory to speak with Mr. Browne. He drove himself the short distance in Tony's curricle, then had the groom drive the horses back to the Priory. With no wish to keep them standing in the cold, he decided he would walk home when his visit was over. He knew Ursula was at the orphanage that day, and he would be able to speak with her father privately.

His reception by Mr. Browne was cordiality itself, but as he made his purpose for being there known, the rector's welcoming smile faded. It was replaced by a look bordering on consternation.

John grew more and more uneasy watching the changing emotions on his host's face. Finally he said bluntly, "I can see you are not pleased with my proposal."

"It's not that, Mr. Hardy. But I fear that Ursula's

response may not be what you hope for. But you may hear for yourself her feelings on the matter. She has come home."

John stepped to where the rector stood near the window. Ursula had tied her gelding to the fence outside the rectory. They heard the outside door open and close; a moment later she stood on the parlor threshold.

She had not seen John Hardy for five days—not since they had argued, and he had kissed her, and she had bolted from Celia's room in her dancing slippers. She could not imagine why he would be in the parlor with her father, and her surprise kept her silent.

"Good afternoon, Miss Browne," John said at his most polite.

"Mr. Hardy," she returned mechanically.

"Yes, well," the rector mumbled. "Mr. Hardy has something he wishes to discuss with you, Ursula, and I have some business to attend to at the church, so if you two will excuse me. It was good talking with you, Mr. Hardy, always a pleasure. Good day to you."

"And to you, sir," John replied as the rector walked briskly from the room and a few moments later was heard leaving the house.

Her father's departure loosed her tongue, and Ursula was the first to speak. "I can't imagine what we can have to discuss. I'm sure we said all there was to say the other night."

"Not quite. Please, Ursula, won't you sit down."

Reminded thus of her bad manners, she asked him to sit, then seated herself near the fire on a petit-point chair worked in a design of scarlet poppies. She folded her hands and remained silent, waiting for him to state his business.

John walked to the window, then turned with his back to it regarding her. "You are not going to make this easy for me, I'm sure, but I have decided to present my position plainly, so there can be no misunderstanding. The other night, when you said you would not be one of my flirts, you mistook my intentions. What I would like, more than anything, would be for you to agree to become my wife."

He had prepared himself for scorn, even anger. He had not expected the bewilderment he now saw in her face, in her whole demeanor.

She was shaking her head in disbelief as she answered, "No. You can't be serious. We're worlds apart. Totally unsuited. You can't know what you're saying."

"I know precisely what I'm saying. I've thought of little else for the past five days. I want you; I always have."

"But you never said anything," she replied accusingly. "You never even hinted; you always treated me like a bratty schoolgirl."

"I never said anything because Wexford warned me off, and because I thought these past couple of years that you were in love with Tony."

She made no direct response to this comment, but said instead, "It can never be, not ever, not between us."

He stepped close and took her shoulders in his hands. "Why do you say that? When I kissed you, you kissed me back. It's the memory of that moment that has given me hope, that has brought me back for more of the same."

She raised her face to his and melted before the fire burning in his eyes. She offered no resistance as he pulled her close and covered her face and lips with kisses. She had drifted into that old dream; indeed, she wallowed there, savoring each moment of a love she knew could never be.

When he finally stopped and put her from him, he expected to see some pleasure or joy in her face. Instead he saw only sorrow. "What is it?" he asked. "Tell me what's wrong."

"When I was ten," she said, "you came to Walsh Priory for the hunting, and I saw you for the first time. I watched you dancing from the gallery above, and I thought you the handsomest man in the world. I fell in love with you then. I remember the first time we were introduced. I remember every word you ever spoke to me. But when I grew older, I learned something that made any hope I ever had of attracting you turn to dust. So I tried to convince myself that you weren't worth having. Recently I was actually starting to believe it."

A pale flush rose to his face as he replied, "If you are alluding to a certain lady in my keeping, I haven't seen her for months, and I swear, I never intended . . . not once I had wed."

"No, John, it's not your mistress, though I had convinced myself you were a villain for keeping her, poor woman. It's not her; it's not you. I am the one who is unworthy, always will be."

"Answer me this," he said. "You loved me at ten; do you love me now?"

"Yes, I do, God help me, though I have tried so often to prove to myself that you are unworthy of my love."

"And you don't love Tony?"

"I do, but with a love of friendship—nothing deeper."

"Then, I can see no impediment."

"You are not listening to me, John. I cannot marry you, not ever."

"Why not?"

She sighed. "I would rather not say, and I would beg you to spare me that final humiliation."

He took her once again by the shoulders forcing her to look at him. "I cannot spare you, nor myself. I must know. Why not?"

"You will hate me when you know, and I will hate you after you have forced me to tell."

"Hate me or love me," he said with feeling, "what difference can it make if you refuse to be my wife?"

He shook her then, impatient with her, and she had the impression that he would not release her until she told him what he wanted to know.

"I am illegitimate, a bastard," she blurted out, "and no fit wife for you, nor for any man who calls himself a gentleman. And nothing you can say will change it, and nothing you can do will ever erase from my memory the look on your face right now. And I will, I *will* hate you forever for making me tell you."

She tore herself from his grasp and ran from the room. So shocked was he by her disclosure that he didn't realize she had left the house until he heard her horse stomping outside. From the window he saw her mount and gallop away.

In mid-December Celia received a letter from her mother. After Melinda had delivered herself of a healthy boy child, Lavinia Demming had packed her trunks and taken herself off to Hereford, where she planned to stay until Sophia's child arrived.

Celia had imagined that her mother would come upon the news of the broken engagement while scanning the society entries, the only portion of a newspaper she was ever known to read. Her mother's letter showed plainly that this had not been the case:

... While I was shopping in Hereford, I encountered the squire's wife, Mrs. Pinchton, nosy busybody that she is. She said to me quite conversationally, "Such a pity about your Celia." Of course, I replied, "What is a pity about Celia?" "Why, her broken engagement," she said. "Such a shame. It would have been a wonderful match for her." Quite beside myself with shock, but not permitted to show it, I said, "Where did you hear about that?" and she replied so smugly, "In the London papers, where else?" Naturally I had to go along with her, so I said, "Certainly it had to be put in, it's the proper thing to do." Pretending I knew all along what was going on, which of course I didn't, because you didn't have the common sense to inform me first before you did such a rash and foolish thing. Never in my life have I been so disappointed in a child of mine. I can't think what possessed you to whistle down the wind that upstanding young man with such excellent connections. You must have gone queer in the attic if you think you will ever find another as fine as Anthony Graydon. I can't think what I would say to you if I should see you now, so perhaps it's best that I must bide here until after the baby arrives. . . .

Celia was not looking forward to her mother's return and the recriminations that would follow, but then Celia wasn't looking forward to much of anything these days. She settled into her old routine, because she couldn't think of anything else to do. She asked her father to arrange the shipment of wool to Pierre Amay, as she had discussed with Lord Wexford.

"I have several business acquaintances in Brussels," he had replied. "I will ship it to one of them and see that it is delivered properly. And I will be certain that someone reads him the letter you wrote."

"And you will send an account along to Lord Wexford, Papa?"

"Certainly I will. If you think I should."

"I do. I think he would expect it. He is a proud and stubborn man. He doesn't like to have debts."

Frederick Demming regarded his daughter with interest. "It seems you came to know Lord Wexford well during your stay at Walsh Priory."

"Yes . . . and no. I thought I knew him, but I didn't, not really. I don't understand men, Papa."

He smiled and put a comforting arm about her

slight shoulders. "Nor do we men understand you ladies. That's what makes it all such a challenge."

"But it's not a challenge for me, Papa. It's confusing, and painful."

"Ah, sweeting, what is it? Tell your papa what it is that saddens you so."

"I wanted to love Tony. I tried. Truly I did. But I couldn't."

"Some marriages do fine without love, Celia, but if you didn't feel that all was as it should be, then you did right to call it off before it was too late."

"Do you truly think so?"

"I do. You're wise to trust your heart, for I think, more often than not, it gives us good counsel."

"Thank you, Papa. It means a lot to me that you understand. I only wish I thought Mama would."

"Don't you worry about your mama. I'll explain it all to her. She won't plague you with it."

Celia wasn't convinced that her mother would be easily mollified. Mostly Papa left the rearing of the girls to his wife, but if he made a promise, he was a man of his word. The few times she had ever heard her parents argue, Papa had always prevailed. She took some comfort from this thought and tried to put the matter from her mind.

Celia had a letter from Emily Crowther saying that she and Kitty had started their lessons together and that they were progressing splendidly. Emily expressed her regret, in the most tactful way, that Celia and Anthony should not be wed after all, but no doubt they knew what was best.

Ursula wrote every week, regular as clockwork. Most of her news was of the orphanage. The shooting party had broken up the week before Christmas, she said. All the guests had gone.

Then, in early January, she wrote to say that old Lord Walsh had died on the first day of the new year. He went quietly in his sleep. Lady Walsh was distraught and refused to leave her rooms.

When she received this news, Celia wrote to Lady Walsh expressing her condolences. She had always admired her ladyship's strength and good sense, and pitied her for her months of hope in a recovery that had not materialized. Tony and Robert would be a great comfort to their mother, of that she was certain.

Mrs. Demming came home at the end of January, when she was satisfied that her daughter and her newest grandson were thriving. She had several lengthy discussions with her husband behind closed doors before she joined Celia one morning in the salon saying they must have a serious talk.

"Your father has put me in possession of the facts concerning your recent . . . your recent dissolution of your commitment to Mr. Graydon. He insists, and I agree, that there is little now that we can do to repair the harm that was done, so we will speak no more about it. There will be plenty of waspish tongues wagging once the Season starts, of that you can be sure. But if we hold to our story, that you and Mr. Graydon mutually decided that you would not suit, we should rub through well enough."

"Were you planning to go to Town for the Season, Mama? You have only just come home."

"Not me, girl. We. You and I. *We* are going to Town for the Season."

"But I can't, Mama. Not now. The last thing I want to do is go back to London."

"It's not a question of what you want to do, Celia, but rather what you must do. If you hide away here in the country, when everyone who is anyone has gone back to Town, people will think you have something to hide, something to be ashamed of."

Celia shook her head in denial, but her mother continued undaunted, "You must be seen everywhere, sparkling, beautiful . . . and available. A bold front is the only thing that will serve us now."

"Mama, please, can't we wait? Go in the fall perhaps for the Little Season. That would be best, I'm sure."

"We leave in two weeks, Celia. I have already ordered the house opened. It is decided. Your papa and I agree. We do not intend to allow you to mope in the country."

Nothing Celia could say would sway her parents from their decision. She thought about running away, but knew there was no place she could go. None of her sisters would shield her if it meant risking Mama's wrath, and she had no other family or friends who would take her in.

The following week, Ursula's letter contained the information that Anthony had taken Lady Walsh abroad for some months. They were to visit Italy and the Greek isles. She felt the change of scenery and sunnier climate would do much to lift Lady Walsh's spirits, which had been quite low since the funeral.

There was a bit of luck for her, Celia thought. At least she wouldn't have to worry about encountering Tony while she was on the Town being "sparkling, beautiful, and available."

Chapter 14

WHEN CELIA CAST herself back into the stream of London society, her reappearance caused very few ripples. If there were those who thought she was quite mad for allowing Anthony Graydon to slip through her grasp, no one said as much to her face.

The timing of her return had also been fortuitous, for the very day that she attended her first public function of the Season, Marianna Otway eloped with Viscount Sands, causing the Town to buzz and the ton to relegate the broken Demming/Graydon engagement to the category of old news.

Celia appeared at party after party. She was beautiful; there was no question that she was available. She said all that was polite, smiled and danced and dined—but the sparkle had gone from her.

One evening in early March, she finished a set of country-dances with Lord Trevanian. He had made it no secret that he was pleased to see her back in Town. He had been her most assiduous suitor during the past several weeks. He returned her, slightly breathless, to her mother's side, where she unfurled her fan and stood for a moment catching her breath.

As her eyes casually swept the room, they stopped suddenly and came to rest on Robert Graydon, now Earl of Walsh, standing not twenty feet from her. As she stared, for he was the last person she expected to see in a crowded London ballroom, she realized that he was staring back at her in the most unsettling way. Not only looking in her direction, but looking directly at her. Gone from his face was the blank indirect gaze of the past. She could hardly believe it was true, but she thought he could actually see her. When he nodded slightly and smiled at her, she was certain.

Despite the strain of their last meeting, she could not hide her pleasure in his recovery, and she smiled and nodded in return.

Robert turned to address a comment to John Hardy, who stood beside him. Celia suspected that John had pointed her out to his cousin.

Robert was much changed. He had gained weight and appeared now, she thought, much as he must have before he went away with the army. He wore a black coat that fitted his broad shoulders smoothly and certainly without the extra space that his clothing had shown in the past. His face had lost its weary hollows and worry lines. He looked healthy, younger, extremely handsome, and somewhat daunting.

She tried to remember the helpless man who had fallen and could not rise from the floor without assistance. He seemed to bear no relation to the self-assured gentleman who stood now at his ease in a crowded, noisy room.

Then before she had time for another thought, he

came toward her, without aid or direction, and stood facing her with no more than two feet between them.

"You can see me," she said.

"I can," he whispered for her ears alone, "and you are more lovely than I imagined."

Choosing to ignore his last words, she asked, "How did you know me?"

"John saw you while you were dancing with Trevanian."

When Mrs. Demming cleared her voice delicately, Celia said immediately, "Allow me, my lord, to introduce my mother, Mrs. Lavinia Demming. This is Lord Walsh, Mama."

"How do you do, my lord," Lavinia replied at her most charming.

"It is a pleasure to meet you, Mrs. Demming. Your daughter has spoken of you often." Then turning back to Celia, he said, "John tells me that the next dance is a waltz you have promised to him. He agreed to let me take his place, if you have no objection."

He raised his brows questioningly as Celia hesitated, then said, "I'm not certain it would be wise, my lord—"

"She would be honored to dance with you, Lord Walsh," Mrs. Demming interjected. "Go, Celia, enjoy yourself."

When he offered his hand, Celia went with him to the edge of the floor where they stood for a moment waiting for the music to begin.

"You are anxious," he said. "Why?"

"Will not people think it strange to see me stand up with you?"

"I don't see why. You had an amicable split with Tony. What better than to be seen to be on good terms with his family? Would you rather I shun you and allow the world to think you have something to be ashamed of?"

"My mother said the same thing when I told her I had no wish to come to Town. She said I should not hide in the country as if I had done something wrong."

"Especially since it was I who was the wrong-doer."

He took her in his arms and turned her onto the floor as the dance began. "Please," she said, "I do not wish to speak of that." Then, adroitly changing the subject, she added, "We were sorry to hear about your father."

"He had a long, full life," he replied. "I saw the note you wrote Mother. That was kind of you."

"Lady Walsh was always good to me. I feel for her in her loss. But tell me about your eyes. When did you regain your sight?"

"I already had light perception back in November during the house party. Images started returning after the new year began. There has been steady progress since then."

"Ursula writes me often. She said nothing."

"I didn't tell anyone until recently. I wanted to be certain it was back to stay and not something temporary."

"And how is your vision now?"

"As good as ever it was."

She smiled. "I'm pleased, so very happy for you. It would have been a tragedy indeed if your sight had never returned."

"All in all," he said, "I think it may have been a blessing in disguise. When you are forced to live without something you value, and then are lucky enough to get a second chance, you are not likely to take it for granted."

Celia made no response to this comment, and they finished the dance in silence. As they walked back toward Mrs. Demming, he said he would give himself the pleasure of calling on Celia in a few days' time.

"I would much rather you didn't," she said coolly. "I'm pleased that your sight has returned, and I wish nothing but the best for you and your family, but I have no desire to renew my acquaintance with you, Lord Walsh. I thought you understood that."

If Robert was offended by this rebuff, he showed no outward sign of it. He accepted her decree with apparent equanimity, saying only, "As you wish, Miss Demming. Good night."

He bowed formally over her hand, then turned and disappeared into the crowd.

John Hardy maintained a comfortable bachelor dwelling in Duke Street, an address he had moved to four years earlier when the first of his three sisters had reached marriageable age. The eldest was now married, but the younger two and his energetic mother were ever present at his family's

Mount Street residence. John much preferred the quiet privacy of this dwelling.

John and Robert sat now in a comfortable salon on the first floor. A fire burned in the grate, occasionally a carriage rattled by on the street outside.

"Will you open your London house?" John asked as he poured brandy and handed it to his cousin.

"Not if you'll have me here."

"You're welcome as long as you like."

"It seems such a bother to have that barrack turned out for me alone. Maybe if Tony comes up later."

"How long will he be on the Continent?"

"He and Mother plan to stay until the end of April."

John sat in an armchair opposite his cousin and propped his feet comfortably upon a footstool. "Don't you think it's time you told me, Rob, why it is you have come to Town?"

For the next week, Celia peered cautiously about the room at every ball or assembly she attended, but saw no sign of Lord Walsh. Then one day, while Mrs. Demming sat with her embroidery and Celia sat with the yarn and needles her mother deplored, a visitor was announced.

Mrs. Demming had discovered that no amount of cajoling would convince Celia to give over knitting socks. Each time a visitor was announced, Lavinia worried what people would think if the news spread about Town that Miss Demming spent her time knitting socks for orphans. Celia had firmly refused to give up this occupation, and Mrs.

189

Demming was forced to wonder what had become of the quiet, biddable child she had sent away to Buckinghamshire a few short months before.

When the Demming butler announced Miss Ursula Browne, Celia leapt to her feet so quickly that her knitting tumbled to the floor unheeded.

"Ursula, what a wonderful surprise!" she exclaimed as she grasped her friend's hand excitedly and led her forward to meet Mrs. Demming.

After the shortest of introductions, during which Mrs. Demming nevertheless was able to take in both the beauty of this young woman and her unfashionable dress, Celia plied Ursula with questions. "What are you doing in London? I had no idea you were coming. How long do you plan to be here? Where are you staying?"

Laughing at Celia's all too obvious delight in seeing her, Ursula tried to answer all the questions at once. "I came to see you; I don't plan to be in London long, and I am staying at a hotel."

"But you can't stay at a hotel. You must come to us. Mustn't she, Mama?"

"Of course, Miss Browne, you must stay here. We shall send a note round to your hotel and have them send your things over straightaway. How many servants have you?"

"Only Millie, my mother's parlormaid. Father refused to let me come alone, so I had to bring her."

"And very right he was," Lavinia concurred. "You would have been foolish indeed to travel alone."

The next hour was consumed with moving Ursula's belongings from the hotel and settling her in the Demming household. Then, while Lavinia stepped out to tea with one of her friends, Celia and Ursula shared theirs in the small back parlor, where they could chat and catch up on all that had happened since they had been apart.

When it came time for Celia to dress for the evening's entertainment, a soiree in Grosvenor Square, she said she wouldn't go. "I will send my excuses, say I have the headache." She didn't suggest that Ursula come along, for they both knew that none of Ursula's gowns would be suitable for a London party.

"Nonsense," Ursula replied. "I want you to go. I am tired from traveling, and I would like to retire early. We will talk tomorrow."

As Celia rose to go upstairs and change, the butler appeared at the door bearing a silver salver upon which reposed a sealed note. "This has just been delivered for you, Miss Demming, by hand. There is a footman in the hall waiting to carry an answer."

Celia took the note and broke the thick wax seal. The message inside was brief:

Miss Demming,
It is imperative that I speak with you on a matter of some importance. I know you have plainly stated your desire not to see me, but I beg of you, for the understanding I feel we once had, to drive with me tomorrow in the park. I could call at ten o'clock if that would be convenient. My man will wait for your reply.

Walsh

"Is it something important?" Ursula asked when she saw the puzzled frown on Celia's face.

"It's an invitation from Lord Walsh to go driving tomorrow morning," she replied, then turned to the butler and said, "Tell his lordship's man that ten o'clock will be fine."

At precisely ten o'clock the following morning, a dashing high-perch phaeton drawn by a handsome pair of grays pulled up before 17 Brook Street. Celia was ready and waiting, her mother more than pleased with her for accepting the invitation. Robert exclaimed when he saw Ursula seated with the Demming ladies in the salon. He said he was delighted to see her in Town and hoped she would enjoy her visit.

When Celia was settled comfortably in the carriage, Robert dismissed his groom, and they set off at a spanking pace for Hyde Park. Celia made no comment about the servant's dismissal since it was obvious they could have no private conversation while he was present.

"Thank you for coming," Robert said.

"I almost said no," she replied honestly. "But the way you worded your note, it would have been churlish to refuse."

"I have all these things I want to say to you," he began. "I've gone over and over it in my mind, and I haven't been able to decide quite how to word it— quite what to say. Sometimes I am convinced I should say nothing at all, simply let you go out of my life, which is what you say you want."

"But I'm not in your life, my lord."

"No. And that's just the point. I want you to be."

"I don't know what you mean."

"I'm not sure I do, either. The only thing I am sure of is that I did massive destruction to our relationship when I kissed you. And I should regret it. But I don't."

"You told me the kiss didn't mean anything to you."

"That was a lie. I said it so that you would think there had been no commitment on my side, so that you would be free to make a choice based on *your* feelings alone. I truly thought you would stay with Tony if you believed there was no attraction on my side."

They entered the park. There were some gentlemen riding but very few carriages at this time of day. Robert allowed his horses to walk at a leisurely pace.

When she said nothing, he continued, "I need to know, and I am praying you will tell me, why you broke your engagement to Tony."

"Didn't he tell you?"

"He said you told him that though you loved him, you were not in love with him."

"That was the truth."

"And was it only a coincidence that you told him this the day after I kissed you?"

"No. It was my attraction to you that made me realize I would be marrying Tony for the wrong reasons. But it made everything much worse that you were his brother, someone he trusted, someone I trusted."

"Is there anything I can do to win back your trust?"

"I don't know. You put me in an untenable position. The last thing I ever wanted to do was keep a secret from my intended husband, but how could I tell him something that would hurt him and at the same time threaten the relationship between the two of you."

"I know. I felt the same way. That's why I told him what happened between us before he left for Italy."

"You told him? How did he react?"

"Not at all the way I expected. Apparently he had done a great deal of soul-searching himself and had come to some conclusions. I thought he would be angry, but he wasn't. He seemed surprised, but said he suspected that something had happened to make you realize you were headed on a course you couldn't finish. He said you pointed out to him that neither of you had verbally pledged your love to the other. He felt you were wise beyond your years for knowing that had meaning. He also said that though he felt you would have had a good and happy marriage, you were probably right in thinking that you both deserved more than merely good and happy."

"He is the most amazing man."

"You'll get no argument from me."

A few moments passed in silence, then he asked, "Would you like to take the reins?"

"No. Thank you. I am enjoying watching you. You must feel wonderfully free to be able to drive again."

"I do. And not only to drive, but to ride and walk. I've spent hours strolling about the Priory grounds looking at things I thought I might never see again. Do you like that carriage rug?"

Celia ran her fingers lightly over the rug the groom had placed carefully across her knees to keep her warm during the drive. "It's lovely, beautifully woven."

"Pierre made it. He sent it several weeks ago along with a letter written for him by a friend of your father's. He was most appreciative of the goods you sent. It was thoughtful of you to remember."

She was surprised. "But we agreed to send them, did we not?"

"We did, but after all that happened, I thought perhaps . . . but I should have known better, for you are a woman of your word."

"I try to be."

"Will you drive with me tomorrow?"

"I can't."

"The next day, then."

"No. Not then, not ever again."

"Celia, you admitted you were attracted to me. Couldn't we give that a chance? See where it leads?"

"It could never work."

"Because of Tony?"

"Because of him, and because of the gossips. I am sick of hearing the whispering that goes on, first after my fall down the stairs and then after my broken engagement. If I gave you the least encouragement now, everyone would say that I had dropped

Tony in order to set my cap at a title—your title. I couldn't bear it. And you are not immune from gossip, either. Would you like it if they whispered that you had cut Tony out in order to secure my dowry for yourself?"

"I think that's unlikely. It's not as if you are an heiress—"

"But I am! My dowry is eighty thousand pounds."

"Good God! How is that possible?"

"I thought you knew. I thought Tony would have told you. Twenty thousand is from my father, the same as my sisters. The other sixty was from my aunt, who was also my godmother, and after whom I was named. She died three years ago and left her entire estate to me."

Suddenly he laughed, but there was no mirth in the sound. "What a tangle!" He pulled the horses to a standstill and turned to face her on the seat. "So what you are telling me is that we should not explore what we felt for each other that day in the maze because we are afraid of a little gossip."

"There's something else," she said quietly.

"What?" he asked, immediately alerted by the tension he heard in her voice.

"I know about Mrs. Drew."

"How could you know?"

"A lot of little things that added up."

"Celia, that all happened a long time ago."

"But you still go to the cottage every Sunday morning."

"I go to see Alan, to spend time with him. Is that so hard to understand?"

She was somewhat relieved to think that it was

the boy and not the beautiful mother that he called regularly to see, but she could not keep the tears from her eyes as she asked, "And you pay for his lessons with the rector, and you keep him on the home farm where you can watch over him and train him one day to be an estate agent?"

"Yes. Those are my plans for him. I feel I owe him that at least. Do you think I should do any less? I wish I could do more."

"But don't you see that it is not all in the past. Alan is very much part of the present."

"You're right. He is a living reminder of a skeleton in the family closet."

"Please try to understand—"

"You don't have to say any more," he interrupted. "I do understand." He started the team again and set them at a trot toward the park gate. "I have tried for the past ten years to safeguard the honor of my family name. But I know, and have always known, that honor once lost is lost forever.

"And there's something else I know, that I wasn't going to tell you, but I think now I will, since I may never get a chance to speak privately with you again. I am in love with you, Celia. I knew it that day in the maze, but I denied it because I wanted what was best for you, and I believed you to be in love with Tony.

"I wish I could tell you that I would send Alan away, and his mother, and any other reminder of the disgrace that descended upon my family the day he was conceived, but I can't do that. I made a promise to myself that I would do everything in my power to right that wrong. And I made that promise long before I knew you."

There was a long silence as he turned the horses into Brook Street. His declaration of love had come like a bolt of lightning from a clear sky. It was the last thing she had ever expected to hear from him. "I don't know what to say to you," she said almost inaudibly.

"You don't have to say anything. I wanted you to know. There is one other thing. My mother doesn't know about Alan and his mother, and it would hurt her a great deal if she did. If you could keep what you've learned in confidence, for her sake, I would be in your debt."

"I won't ever say anything. I promise."

Robert's groom was waiting at the house when they pulled up, and he ran to hold the horses. Robert alighted, then reached up to help Celia. He kept her hand a moment after she was safely down. "If you ever need a friend, anytime, for any reason, I hope you'll think of me."

Chapter 15

URSULA AND CELIA were together in the sitting room busy with their needlework. For once Celia was occupied with what her mother considered an appropriate task. She was monogramming handkerchiefs for her father. Lavinia had gone down to Richmond to spend two days with her sister. Celia had declined the invitation, saying she would be happy to have a few quiet days at home to visit with Ursula.

"You wrote me that the orphanage near your home was inadequate," Ursula said, "but you didn't go into detail. What was it like?"

"It was dreadful. More like a stable than a suitable home for children. There were very few windows, and the ones there were, were small and dirty, with no curtains or coverings of any kind. The woman in charge was slovenly and lazy. The only fireplaces were downstairs where the matron and other adults slept. The only heat the children got was what happened to seep upstairs between the cracks in the floorboards. I went with my father the first time, and he refused to let me go again until the place had been cleaned up a bit."

"How did you accomplish that?"

"The building was on a piece of property belonging to Lord Sewell, who is by good fortune a friend of my father's. We convinced his lordship that the woman in charge would be better off elsewhere and found a widow from the village, whose children are grown, who was interested in taking on the project. My father and Lord Sewell both sent over some men to work, and in a very short space of time they had swept out all the dirt and grime, cleaned the windows, patched the walls, and mended broken glass. Then everything got a fresh whitewashing. I couldn't believe how much brighter it was when I was permitted to go again.

"At about this stage of the process, my eldest sister, Amelia, who is married to Lord William Lane, began to take an interest in the work we were doing there. Her husband donated brick and masons to build new chimneys and install fireplaces in each dormitory. He even agreed to supply coal for heating. Then Amelia began to gather volunteers from the neighborhood—men to teach the boys crafts, and women to teach the girls to sew and cook. Everyone has been so generous with their time and money. I don't think they ever meant to ignore the plight of those poor children; I just think they never knew how bad it was for them."

"So Amelia is watching over all in your absence?"

"Yes. She was wonderful. When Mama insisted I come to Town, Amelia said I should go, for she would see that all our plans went forward."

"You would be pleased with the progress Kitty is

making with both her reading and writing," Ursula said.

"Yes, I know. I saw Emily Crowther last week at the opera. She said she was grateful that you could take over for her and that she would relieve you of the task when she comes home at the end of May."

"I was more than happy to do it. Kitty is such a biddable child." Ursula stood up suddenly, set her knitting aside, and walked restlessly to the window. "That's not entirely true. What I really wanted to do was come up to Town like you and Emily so that I could be close to John, see him again."

"John Hardy?"

"Yes. A day or so after you left the Priory last November, he asked me to marry him."

Celia clapped her hands together, her embroidery forgotten. "I knew it! I knew he cared for you! And you admire him, too, despite the way you fuss and fume at each other."

"I did not accept him."

"But, Ursula, why not?"

"It's a long story. I have been longing to confide in someone. I almost went to Robert, but I'm relatively certain I know what he would say. I wanted a female opinion. I trust you to give me honest advice and keep my secret."

Then, while a chill rain fell outside the sitting room windows, Ursula poured out the whole story: how she and John had argued the night of the party at Walsh Priory, how he had later proposed, how she had admitted loving him, and finally how she had driven him away with her confession of illegitimacy.

As Celia listened, her heart went out to her friend. She realized that all these months, while she had been heartsore over her break with Tony and her feelings for Robert, thinking she must be the most miserable woman in the world, Ursula had been suffering in a similar fashion.

"What did he say," Celia asked, "when you finally told him the reason you wouldn't marry him?"

"He didn't say anything. He just looked at me . . . and, my God, I will never forget that look. Never, not as long as I live."

The door opened, and a maid carried in the tea tray. No sooner had she departed than the butler entered to announce two visitors.

"At this hour, Walker? I didn't invite anyone for tea."

"It is Lord Walsh, miss, and Mr. Hardy."

This announcement brought both women to their feet as the men entered the room and offered cordial greetings. Both gentlemen were dressed in dark coats, pale pantaloons, and shiny Hessians. Robert's face was a study in anxiety.

"Shall I bring more tea, miss?" Walker asked.

"Yes, certainly. Please, gentlemen, won't you be seated?"

As soon as the door closed behind Walker, Celia protested, "This is highly irregular, my lord."

To give him credit, Robert both looked and sounded apologetic. He nodded at his cousin. "I tried to stop him. But he would come. I thought I had best come along rather than let him burst in here on his own."

"Ursula," John said. "I must speak with you. I

202

have been badgering Robert since he told me you were in Town, but he refuses to give me any information. He insists my answers must come from you. Is there someplace we can talk privately?"

When he cast a meaningful glance at Celia, Ursula said, "Celia knows the conditions of my birth, and she also knows that I have refused your suit. There is nothing you can say to me that she and Robert cannot hear."

"Very well. If you had opened any one of the letters I sent you during the winter, instead of returning them unopened, you would know that my offer of marriage still stands, despite what you call the 'conditions of your birth.' I don't care *who* or *what* your father was; I don't even care if you don't *know* who he was. I am in love with *you.*"

"But I care, John, don't you see?"

"Yes, I do see, but we can't change what has happened in the past. We can only start with what we have today and build for the future."

Walker arrived with another tea tray and conversation lagged while he was in the room. When he had gone again, Robert said, "I think we should build up the fire and make ourselves comfortable. Then, with Ursula's permission, I would like to tell you, John, and you, too, Celia, who Ursula's father is, for we do indeed know who he is."

He cast a questioning look at Ursula. "Go ahead," she said. "Tell them. Tell them everything you know. And if there is anything you haven't yet told me, I would like to hear that, too."

John sat near Ursula on a small sofa and took

one of her hands in his. Robert and Celia sat on a facing sofa, close, but not touching.

"Ursula," Robert began, "is my sister. To be precise, she is my half sister. She is also Tony's half sister. We all three share the same father. You were right, John, when you detected her feelings for Tony and for me. Only they weren't quite the kind of feelings you thought they were.

"Lest I should now be accused of speaking ill of the dead, let me say that the words I am about to speak, I would say to my father's face if he were alive, and in fact, did say to him on more than one occasion.

"When he was a man in his late forties, he saw, and lusted after, Eleanor Bates, who is now Eleanor Browne, Ursula's mother. She was a young girl not yet twenty, the daughter of the village doctor. My father was lord of the manor—handsome, wealthy, powerful. She has told me herself that she loved him, and believed he loved her, and gave herself to him because of that love.

"When Eleanor became pregnant, the doctor was one of the first to notice. When he demanded of my father that something be done to save his daughter's reputation, my father paid a young cleric, who had recently taken orders and had no position, to marry the girl and pass the child off as his own.

"This poor, but nonetheless worthy, man was our own Mr. Browne, who married Eleanor and took her to a living in Sussex, arranged for him by my father. As part of their bargain, the living here in Little Graydon was promised to Mr. Browne as soon as it became vacant. The vacancy occurred when Ursula was about eight. The Brownes moved to Little Graydon, and Ursula lived in the shadow of her father's house. No one suspected that the Brownes' lovely child was anything other than she appeared to be.

"When all this first began, I was only eight years old and, of course, had no notion of what had occurred. But the year Ursula turned sixteen, that changed. I was then twenty-five, and Tony twenty-three. Mrs. Browne came to me that summer and told me her story. She said that now that Ursula was of an age, and knowing how young people could be attracted to one another, she thought it imperative for the three of us, Tony and Ursula and I, to know of our blood relationship. She feared my father would not have told us. She had guessed correctly, of course; he had said nothing. I told Tony almost immediately, and after some consultation, Mrs. Browne and I told Ursula."

He looked at her now. The tears she had been holding back with difficulty suddenly overflowed. He pulled a handkerchief from his pocket and handed it to her, smiling at her fondly. "I remember so clearly how heartbroken you were that day, not because you fully realized at sixteen what your illegitimacy meant, but because you learned that your dear father, the only father you had ever known, was not your father at all."

When he finally stopped talking, Celia asked Robert, "If you and John are first cousins, are John and Ursula related?"

"No. John's father is my mother's brother. There is no blood relation between John and Ursula."

John put an arm around Ursula's shoulders, pulling her against his chest. "You're the daughter of an earl, my dear," he said, looking down into her tearstained face. "That's better breeding than I have."

"It's no breeding at all when you're a bastard," she insisted.

"Do you think that every man in the country who calls himself a gentleman is legitimate? Some of our leading families recognize illegitimate offspring. Look at Devonshire. Ursula, you're gently born. No blame should attach to you for the mistakes of your parents."

Turning his attention to his cousin, John asked, "Who knows about this? About who her real parents are?"

"The four of us here, Ursula's parents, and Tony. No one else. My mother never knew."

"But other people could find out." Ursula said.

John took both her hands and turned her on the sofa to face him. "How? No one here will ever tell, and there's no way anyone else could discover it. I want you for my wife, Ursula, and if you won't marry me, I will never marry."

Ursula turned confused eyes to Celia. "What do you think I should do?"

"I think you should follow your heart and forget about your birth," Celia replied. "Why should you spend the rest of your life paying for your father's mistake?"

Ursula looked to Robert. "I agree with Celia," he said. "If John has no doubts or reservations, then you need have none, either. John loves you for who you are and what you are today, and if you love him the same way, then you should be together."

When John took Ursula into his arms once again, Robert rose to his feet, took Celia by the hand, and led her to the far side of the room. They sat in a large bay window with a padded seat facing the garden behind the house. Having moved behind the high-backed sofa where Ursula and John sat, they couldn't see the other couple at all. Nor could they distinguish the words that came to them as a soft murmur.

The steady rain pattered against the windowpanes and ran in rivulets down the glass. Robert collected a warm shawl from a chair and draped it about Celia's shoulders.

"There's a chill here by the window, but they need some privacy, and we can't leave them alone." Celia remained silent, and in the light from a candelabra on the table nearby, he saw her regarding him with a troubled expression on her face. "Why do you look at me like that?"

"You're always surprising me," she replied. "When I think I am beginning to understand you, you do something totally unexpected."

"Like what?"

"The way you were just now with Ursula. So loving and understanding, seeing everything so clearly and stating the facts plainly."

"But I do love Ursula. And the facts are plain, though admittedly sometimes hard to see through pain."

When she still looked troubled, he prodded, "What else?"

"Earlier, when you spoke of your father, it sounded as if you despised him."

"I despised his behavior, it's true. Can you blame me? His careless need to satisfy his own desire at the expense of others has led to a great deal of unhappiness."

"But how can you judge his behavior so harshly, when you have followed so closely in his footsteps? Done the same thing. Hurt people even as he did."

"I have? How?"

"You know how. With Mrs. Drew and her son."

"I know they've been hurt, but not through any fault of mine. I have done all I could." When she looked skeptical, he asked defensively, "What more would you have me do?"

"You should have married her when she discovered she was increasing. You were single at the time, you had not your father's excuse that he already had a wife."

"*I* should have married Harriet?" he asked, his voice incredulous.

"Yes, you should have. Both to take responsibility for your actions and to give your son your name."

"Give my son?—What on earth are you talking about, Celia? Alan is not my son. He is my father's child, and like Ursula, my half sibling. You thought he was *my* son?"

"Mrs. Forbes told me he was."

"That old gossip! And you believed her?"

"Well, I had already realized that you took special notice of the boy. And I knew that you called regularly to visit Mrs. Drew."

"Next you will say you thought she was my mistress," he replied caustically.

"Actually I did think she was, but when you told me the other day that you only went there to see the boy, I believed you."

"Oh, thank you very much," he mocked. "How long have you been regarding me in this flattering light?"

"Since a few days before I left Walsh Priory. I visited with Mrs. Forbes the same day I made my last trip to the orphanage. She told me then."

"Told you what, exactly?"

"That everyone in the village knew that Mr. Drew was not Alan's father. That Alan had your eyes and voice."

"How can everyone in the village know something that isn't true? Did it never occur to you that I have my *father's* eyes and voice?"

"No, why should it. He was a frail old man, bedridden—"

"So it was much easier to think the worst of me."

"Mrs. Forbes doesn't think badly of you. She said young men would be wild, and things happen."

"I would like to tell Mrs. Forbes a thing or two, and perhaps shall when I get home. Old men can be wild, too, and my father was among the worst. Until a few years ago he was a striking man, tall, quite handsome, obviously virile. God knows how many bastards he sired about the countryside. Ursula and Alan are the only two I know about, but I am willing to bet there are more."

"How did you learn about Alan?" she asked.

"Harriet and I were friends, close to the same

age. She came to me when she discovered she was pregnant. She was actually considering suicide—said she could never hold up her head again once her shame was discovered.

"I thought of George Drew. I had met him at the Newmarket races when I was about seventeen. I invited him here several times during school holidays. His father was a solicitor in Norwich, and George was planning to be the same. He knew Harriet from the times he had stayed here; I knew he admired her. I wrote to him, explained the situation. He said he would marry her if she would have him. They were wed the following week. She had trouble with the birth and could never have another child, but George loved that boy as his own, and he loved Harriet, too. It was a good marriage.

"It was nearly six years later that I found out about Ursula. I never doubted Mrs. Browne's story, for I already had my father's measure."

Celia reached out to touch his wrist, and he turned his hand over to take hers in a warm clasp. "I can't tell you," she said, "how sorry I am that I gave any credence to Mrs. Forbes. It was foolish of me, because I know better than most how destructive gossip can be."

"Maybe you wanted to think ill of me."

She looked shocked at such a suggestion. "Why would I want that?"

"Because it made it easier to walk away, easier to forget what you felt when I kissed you." He took her face gently between his hands and kissed her

210

as he had that day in the maze, slowly and deliberately.

And Celia experienced again what she had known that day, the all-consuming warmth, the mesmerizing passion. She felt that she would be content to stay right there in his arms forever. When he finally freed her mouth, she whispered somewhere between joy and tears, "I love you, Robert."

He immediately held her away so he could look into her face. "Oh, do you, now?" he said with such a twinkle in his eye and such a glow of happiness that her heart turned over. "One moment I'm the evil ogre, besmircher of innocent women, and the next I'm beloved. How can this be?"

"I loved you even when I thought you were a besmircher of innocent women," she said. "That's why I was so unhappy."

He took her hands and kissed them, then held them together between his. "Celia, will you marry me?" When a cloud instantly crossed her face, he said, "Forget the gossips. We won't let them worry us. Should we both be unhappy for the rest of our days because we care what nosy busybodies think?"

"I don't care about them, but I care about Tony."

"Tony will understand. In fact, I think he understood long before we did. So what do you say? Will you marry me?"

"Yes." Then at his gleam of victory she added quickly, "But not soon. And we cannot announce our engagement until Tony knows first. I won't have him reading about it in an outdated London paper, or hearing it secondhand from some traveling gossip-monger."

"I have a better plan," he said. "We will be married as soon as possible, by special licence, in deference to my family's recent bereavement. We will travel to the Continent, where we will join Tony and Mother and tell them personally of our marriage. Then we will go off on our own for several weeks of honeymoon in the Greek isles. Afterward, we can return to London as a family, all of us together, showing one united front. How does that sound to you?"

Then, without giving her an opportunity to answer, he kissed her again. "Unless, of course, you want a big, formal wedding," he said, "which I know every woman wants."

"I don't want a big, formal wedding, Robert. I only want you."

Lavinia Demming had decided to cut short her visit to her sister in Richmond. If she hurried, she would be home in time to dress Celia for Almack's. Lord Trevanian would be there—and perhaps Lord Walsh. He had waltzed with Celia, then surprisingly taken her driving. This behavior had given Lavinia food for thought.

When the butler relieved her of her cloak in the front hall, she said, "Is Miss Celia home, Walker?"

"Yes, madam. She and Miss Browne are in the sitting room."

More to herself than to him, Lavinia muttered, "Good. I must speak with her."

As she stepped toward the sitting room doors,

Walker spoke again, "The young ladies are not alone, madam. They are entertaining callers."

"At this time of day? Who?"

"The Earl of Walsh and Mr. John Hardy."

Lavinia's eyebrows rose with interest. "John Hardy is Walsh's first cousin, I believe," she said, once again thinking aloud. "How long have the gentlemen been here, Walker?"

"They came at teatime."

A quick glance at the hall clock showed Lavinia that it was well past five o'clock. "That's more than an hour, Walker! What can they be talking about so long?"

"I can't say, madam. When I went in to collect the tea things, Miss Browne and Mr. Hardy were seated near the fire. Miss Celia and his lordship were sharing the window seat."

Without another word, Lavinia turned and sailed off toward the sitting room, a smile as broad as the Thames upon her face.